Our Texas Cattleman's
mission to

Tricky and dangerous, D
on the loose, and no one will be safe until this
villain is safely behind bars!

This month in
FIT FOR A SHEIKH
by Kristi Gold

Meet Darin Shakir—
expert tracker and brooding man of mystery. He's
determined to complete his mission on his own.
But that's before he winds up in Fiona Powers's
bed…and she finds her way into his heart!

SILHOUETTE DESIRE
IS PROUD TO PRESENT THE

**Six wealthy Texas bachelors—all members of the
state's most exclusive club—must unravel the
mystery surrounding one tiny baby…and
discover true love in the process!**

So join us as our sexy heroes bring this series to a
satisfying, sensual conclusion….

Dear Reader,

Welcome back to another passionate month at Silhouette Desire. A *Scandal Between the Sheets* is breaking out as Brenda Jackson pens the next tale in the scintillating DYNASTIES: THE DANFORTHS series. We all love the melodrama and mayhem that surrounds this Southern family— how about you?

The superb Beverly Barton stops by Silhouette Desire with an extra wonderful title in her bestselling series THE PROTECTORS. *Keeping Baby Secret* will keep *you* on the edge of your seat—and curl your toes all at the same time. What would you do if you had to change your name and your entire history? Sheri WhiteFeather tackles that compelling question when her heroine is forced to enter the witness protection program in *A Kept Woman*. Seems she was a kept woman of another sort, as well...so be sure to pick up this fabulous read if you want the juicy details.

Kristi Gold has written the final, fabulous installment of THE TEXAS CATTLEMAN'S CLUB: THE STOLEN BABY series with *Fit for a Sheikh*. (But don't worry, we promise those sexy cattlemen with be back.) And rounding out the month are two wonderful stories filled with an extra dose of passion: Linda Conrad's dramatic *Slow Dancing With A Texan* and Emilie Rose's supercharged *A Passionate Proposal*.

Enjoy all we have to offer this month—and every month— at Silhouette Desire.

Melissa Jeglinski

Melissa Jeglinski
Senior Editor, Silhouette Desire

Please address questions and book requests to:
Silhouette Reader Service
U.S.: 3010 Walden Ave., P.O. Box 1325, Buffalo, NY 14269
Canadian: P.O. Box 609, Fort Erie, Ont. L2A 5X3

Fit for a Sheikh

KRISTI GOLD

Published by Silhouette Books
America's Publisher of Contemporary Romance

Special thanks and acknowledgment are given to Kristi Gold for her contribution to the TEXAS CATTLEMAN'S CLUB series.

To editor Stephanie Maurer and authors Sara, Laura, Kathie, Cindy and Cathleen for making participation in this TCC series such a pleasurable experience!

 SILHOUETTE BOOKS

ISBN 0-373-76576-2

FIT FOR A SHEIKH

Books by Kristi Gold

Silhouette Desire

Cowboy for Keeps #1308
Doctor for Keeps #1320
His Sheltering Arms #1350
Her Ardent Sheikh #1358
*Dr. Dangerous #1415
*Dr. Desirable #1421
*Dr. Destiny #1427
His E-Mail Order Wife #1454
The Sheikh's Bidding #1485
*Renegade Millionaire #1497
Marooned with a Millionaire #1517
Expecting the Sheikh's Baby #1531
Fit for a Sheikh #1576

*Marrying an M.D.

KRISTI GOLD

has always believed that love has remarkable healing powers and feels very fortunate to be able to weave stories of romance and commitment. As a bestselling author and a Romance Writers of America RITA® Award finalist, she's learned that although accolades are wonderful, the most cherished rewards come from the most unexpected places, namely from personal stories shared by readers. Kristi resides on a ranch in Central Texas with her husband and three children, along with various and sundry livestock. She loves to hear from readers and can be contacted at KGOLDAUTHOR@aol.com or P.O. Box 9070, Waco, TX 76714.

"What's Happening in Royal?"

NEWS FLASH, April—Looks like all the action is happening in Las Vegas these days! Alexander Kent just returned with his beautiful bride, Stephanie, in tow. What started off as a surprise engagement seems to have exploded into a passionate romance while they were in Vegas. The sparks that couple is giving off are enough to start a grass fire!

Sheikh Darin Shakir has recently been spotted in Vegas, as well…. Our roving reporter, on track of just what went down there, has informed us that this mysterious Cattleman's Club member was last seen in the company of a very sexy redhead. Darin is yummy enough to make any woman fall for him, but our reporter seems to think there was something more going on than a simple fling in Sin City.

There's plenty of hubbub in town since the dangerous Dr. Birkenfeld escaped last month. The sheriff was fit to be tied when he found out and the words he spewed at our reporters were just not suitable for this paper! No one knows exactly where Birkenfeld may be…or when he may come back. Our favorite gents at the Texas Cattleman's Club are still avoiding an interview, but it is clear they're worried. Come on, guys. Can we catch the baddie so that this crowd can have a true happily-ever-after?

One

Men viewed him as a dangerous loner who would stop at nothing in the search for justice. Women considered him a compelling lover who would stop at nothing in the pursuit of pleasure. A dark prince. Enigmatic. Invincible.

As a former military tracker, tempting fate and defying fear had become a way of life for Sheikh Darin ibn Shakir. A means to escape his own demons and a noble legacy he had never embraced. Yet the mission he was about to undertake had resurrected past failures he would rather forget. But he couldn't forget, not this time. Not until he saw the murderous Dr. Roman Birkenfeld—who had stolen infants from their mothers then sold them as if they were his to barter—punished for his heinous crimes. Whatever it might take.

Preparing for his departure to Las Vegas, Darin began filling the black duffel bag with supplies and clothing he would need for his travels. He paused momentarily to survey the room where he'd resided over the past year. His cousin, Hassim "Ben" Rassad, had welcomed him into his home and facilitated Darin's membership into the elite Texas Cattleman's club, a group of men who assisted in apprehending criminals few would dare to confront. Although Darin was grateful for the opportunities, he planned to move on to the next mission alone, tracking an extremist in Obersburg who had threatened the royal family. He had no ties in America aside from his older brother, Raf, who resided in Georgia, and Ben. As for his homeland, Amythra, he'd vowed to never return. The place held nothing but bitter memories.

"The car is on its way."

Darin turned toward the door to find his cousin dressed in faded jeans and scuffed cowboy boots that gave no indication he, too, had been born into nobility. Glancing at the lone bag set on the end of the bed, Ben asked, "Is that all you are taking?"

"I do not anticipate remaining for more than a few days."

"You should pack this, as well."

Darin afforded a cursory glance at the square of white cloth and gold band Ben held out to him. "I have no need for a kaffiyeh where I am going." He'd had no need for any royal trappings for some time now. Ben's brother, Kalib, ruled as king of Amythra, therefore Darin was far down the line in terms of inheriting the throne. A good thing because he did not want that burden. He never had.

Ben offered the kaffiyeh again. "You could use it as a disguise, if for no other reason."

Seeing no need to argue that point, Darin took the kaffiyeh from Ben and stuffed it inside the bag's outer pocket.

"Alexander Kent tells me he has arranged assistance from the Bureau," Ben said.

Something else that did not please Darin, although he greatly respected Alex Kent, a former FBI agent and fellow Cattleman's Club member. "I would prefer to work alone."

Ben released a frustrated sigh. "Might I remind you that when you joined our organization, you agreed to work with the others as a team?"

Darin needed no reminders. He'd been working that way

for the past year, and he'd had no difficulty adhering to the policy. But this was different. This was personal. "I did not realize that this assignment would include other branches of law enforcement."

"It is necessary since this mission does not involve private hire. The illegal adoption ring and extortion violated federal law. That is the way in this country."

"I will honor the law. I will also have Birkenfeld in custody in a matter of days."

Ben looked skeptical. "Do you really believe you will find him so quickly?"

Darin holstered the Beretta, secured the strap over his shoulder then slipped a black jacket over his T-shirt and the gun. "Birkenfeld is not as smart as he believes, even if he did escape the authorities." And that thought brought about Darin's anger. He had been involved in the doctor's original capture, only to have the criminal slip through their hands due to Birkenfeld's cunning and desperation and one novice police officer's inadvertent mistake.

"Then you are certain he is still in Las Vegas?" Ben asked.

Normally Darin would be guarded with that information, something else he had pledged when he'd joined the Cattleman's Club. But Ben was still officially a member, though he'd retired from active missions since his marriage. Therefore, Darin had no reason to withhold details in the case. "He is there, according to the attorney, Larry Sutter, Birkenfeld's cohort. Birkenfeld contacted Sutter on his cell phone and arranged a meeting in some obscure Las Vegas lounge. I am to join an operative posing as a bartender."

"This Sutter is in Las Vegas, as well?"

"Yes, in a hospital under protective custody since he has decided to turn state's evidence in exchange for a lesser sentence. It appears he will be there for a while as he recovers from Kent's beating."

"Alexander Kent beat him?" Shock reflected in Ben's tone and expression.

"He was protecting his lover from Sutter while they were

infiltrating the adoption ring. There are no limits to what a man will do for the woman he loves.'' Even kill if necessary, something Darin knew intimately.

Ben sent him a knowing look. "Very true. I, too, have been in that position."

So had Darin, yet he had failed where Ben had not.

Ben thrust his hands in his pockets and watched while Darin took a few more things from the bureau drawers and added them to the bag. Darin sensed his cousin wanted to say something more, and not necessarily anything he wanted to hear.

"Are you certain you should be the one undertaking this particular mission?" Ben asked, confirming Darin's suspicions.

"I volunteered. Unlike the other members involved, I have no wife with whom to be concerned." No one waiting for him. No one who really worried over his activities.

"It is past time for you to consider settling down, Darin. Past time you find a suitable woman to share in your life."

After stuffing the last of his clothing into the bag, Darin zipped it with a vengeance. "I have no desire to settle down. After Raf's wife died, I decided my brother and I are cursed when it comes to women."

Ben's smile was cynical. "I thought you were too logical to believe in curses."

"I was, before…" Before his world had come apart with the speed of a bullet.

"Before you lost her," Ben finished for him. "Yes, the outcome was tragic, but we are all fortunate, and grateful, that you stopped Habib before he did further harm. You had no control over the situation beyond that."

"I do not care to take the risk with another woman. Not with the life I choose to lead."

"Yet you risk your life much of the time. Why not take a chance on finding a wife? I did, and I have no regrets."

Darin recognized that Ben had found a very special woman, someone worth that risk. An American woman whose determination and spirit equaled most men Darin had known. He could not blame his cousin for falling for Jamie. She was everything a man would desire in a life partner, beautiful and full of passion. Ben and Jamie's commitment and love for each other was obvious in every look they exchanged, a painful reminder of what Darin had once had—and lost—and one of the reasons why he needed to leave their home. The other reason cried, "Papa! Papa!" as she rushed into the room and grabbed Ben around the legs, her light brown hair flowing over her tiny shoulders.

Ben picked up two-and-a-half-year-old Lena and lifted her high above his head, much to the little girl's delight. "You are full of energy today, *yáahil*." He brought her into his arms and kissed her cheek. "I thought you were making *xúbuz* with your mother and Alima."

Lena wrinkled her upturned nose. "I don't like bread. I want cookies." She sent Darin a vibrant smile, much like her mother's, then pointed to his chin. "Scratchies all gone, Dawin?" she asked, as always mispronouncing his name, something Darin found endearing.

Ignoring the deep ache radiating from his heart, he rubbed his clean-shaven jaw and favored her with a smile. "Yes, little one. All gone down the drain." He'd removed the goatee that morning to make himself less recognizable to Birkenfeld. He had also cut his hair to the top of his collar and now wore a gold loop in each ear. Hopefully enough of a change to disguise himself somewhat, which brought about a reminder of something he had almost forgotten.

Darin tucked his hair behind his ears and set the black baseball cap low on his forehead. He then picked up the bag and said, "I am ready."

Lena leveled her dark eyes on him. "Where ya goin', Dawin?"

He walked to her and ran a fingertip over her soft cheek. "To a place with many bright lights." And a man who needed to be tracked down and punished.

She leaned over and touched his jaw as if fascinated with the absence of whiskers. "I wanna go."

Darin took her hand and kissed her palm. "Not this time, little one."

As Darin, Ben and Lena headed through the great room, Jamie met them at the front door. "Leaving again, Darin?"

"For a time."

Jamie raked a hand through her blond hair and patted her distended abdomen. "I hope you'll be back in the next few days for the baby's birth. It's really something to see big tough Ben here in nervous father mode. I swear, I thought he was going to pass out when Lena—"

Ben halted her words with a kiss, then wrapped his arm around her shoulder. "I was quite calm during Lena's birth."

Jamie grinned and Lena giggled. "If you say so, honey."

True affection passed between father, mother and child, evidenced by shared smiles, Lena's head resting against Ben's chest, Jamie's arm around Ben's waist.

Needing to escape, Darin walked onto the porch, thankful to discover the sedan had arrived to take him to the airstrip. Seeing this closely bound family was almost too much for him to bear, although he would never reveal that to anyone.

Before entering the car, he turned to wave goodbye, and little Lena with her father's eyes and her mother's smile, blew him a kiss.

Memories of what might have been crowded Darin's mind, save for one cruel bastard who had taken three lives—Ben's father, Darin's fiancée and their unborn child. A man much like Dr. Roman Birkenfeld. Both had no regard for the sanctity of life and the rare gift of love.

Darin vowed to hunt down Birkenfeld even if it proved to be his last act on earth. But in the process, Sheikh Darin ibn Shakir would not allow himself to feel his own pain. Not if he wanted to succeed.

Not much went on in the off-the-strip Silver Ace Lounge on Mondays. The absolute height of boredom, a familiar concept for Fiona Powers. Hotel management student by day, bartender by night, the same-old, same-old since she'd moved to Vegas from Idaho five years before. But no one had said life would be easy for a struggling small-town gal with big-time dreams.

Fiona slapped a rag over the counter where some drunk had missed his big mouth, pouring his boilermaker all over himself and the bar. Fiona had tried to cut him off after two rounds, but scrawny, balding Benny Jack, the other barkeep, had kept on serving the guy as if he'd been doling out fruit juice. Thankfully, the inebriate had left an hour ago after Fiona had called him a cab, as well as some unflattering names under her breath.

"Slow night, huh, Fee-Fee?"

Fiona turned and leaned back against the bar, elbows braced on the counter, preparing to repeat the same admonishments to Benny Jack. "For the thousandth time, Fee-Fee is the name someone would give a poodle, and I assure you I am not a poodle even if my hair is curly. I do not sit up on my hind legs and beg, nor do I leave puddles on the sidewalk. But if I were a canine, I would take great pleasure in planting my pointy little teeth in the middle of your butt. Better still, I would probably go directly for the nethers and give them a good shake."

Benny grinned, displaying his lack of teeth. "Didn't know you were into that kinky stuff, Red."

Red. The second-worst nickname Fiona had encountered. Obviously Benny was determined to cut his life short tonight. "Don't you have somewhere to be? Maybe some cave on the other side of the continent?"

Benny hooked his thumbs in his suspenders. "Yep. I got a date."

Great. Benny, the toothless, thin man had a date and Fiona was stuck tending regulars in a dive. "Just some advice, Benny. When you pick her up, don't drag her by the hair to your car."

Benny grinned again before turning toward the exit. "By the way, a new guy's coming in to relieve you in a while."

"What new guy?" Fiona said but received no response since Benny had already left out the back door to commence with his courting ritual that probably involved a back-seat roll with some big-haired broad.

And here she was, faced with a new guy no one had bothered to tell her about, not even Jimmy, the bar's owner. Oh well, at least she might get home early to do some studying. *If* the latest employee knew how to tend bar. Otherwise, she'd have to train him, and hopefully that didn't require newspaper on the floor. Jimmy had a tendency to hire knuckle-scraping morons—case in point, Benny Jack.

Fiona turned back to survey the limited occupants—two middle-aged guys in polyester pants shooting pool and bull, and one elderly man reading the paper and smoking a fat cigar that smelled about as delightful as stagnant sewage.

She leaned over the bar, propped her cheek on her palm and sighed. Yeah, just another night in nonparadise. But what could she expect when she chose to work in a place that served as stomping grounds for locals with the mean age of sixty? At least the tips were good, but for once she wished someone more interesting would come in.

The front door opened, and she expected another of life's little disappointments to enter in the form of an octogenarian. What she got was the surprise of her life.

He seemed to emerge from the smoky haze like some otherworldly presence who had recently landed from Planet Machismo where the all-male aliens survived on testosterone alone. He wore black, from his baseball cap to his combat boots. Black cargo pants, black T-shirt, black jacket— Jacket? No one wore a jacket in Vegas in April, unless they were hiding something or hiding from someone. He stalked toward the bar with confidence as if challenging someone to stop his progress, his dark gaze scanning the room.

Fiona's hopes soared when she considered he might be the new bartender. They dropped when he slid onto the stool with the prowess of a panther, directly in front of Fiona like any other customer. He studied her as if he expected her to swoon. She wasn't going to do that, although her knees did feel a little flimsy.

She sent him a smile. "What can I get for you?" Coffee? Tea? Me?

"Coffee."

Darn. "Black?"

"Yes."

This did not surprise Fiona, nor did the fact that his voice was deep as a water well. She had never seen such a perfectly chiseled face covered by skin the color and texture of melted milk chocolate. Obviously black was his signature color, right down to the shadow of whiskers framing his full lips and the long dark lashes outlining his eyes, which Fiona considered totally unfair. Her lashes showed up after applying two coats of mascara. A slight indentation to the right of the bridge of his straight nose, as if it had been broken at one time, was the only true flaw in his face. But it sure as heck didn't detract from his incredible looks.

Forcing her gaze away, Fiona turned from the counter to the back shelf housing the coffeepot and realized the temperature had just risen about a hundred degrees. She poured some of the muddy brew into the mug, glanced in the mirrored wall, then tightened the band securing her hair high on her head as if that would improve her appearance. Her ponytail looked like a spastic bird's nest, random tendrils falling around her face like loose springs. Her sleeveless blue blouse revealed the results of happy hour and displayed all the freckles on her pale arms. Just her luck. Hank the Hunk had walked into her life and she looked like warmed-over deer dung.

Fiona gripped the cup in both hands, hoping it didn't slide across the damp surface and land in his lap when she set it down. Of course, then she would be forced to hop over the bar and clean it up, not an altogether unpleasant thought. But hot coffee on his crotch did not a good impression make, not to mention it might be painful if it seeped through his pants. Then he would have to take his pants off—

Earth to Fiona.

She turned back to the bar and set the cup before him, fortunately without incident. "It's kind of strong."

He kept his intense eyes fixed on hers. "I prefer it that way."

He might as well have said he preferred randy sex, considering the way Fiona's body reacted with a series of hot flashes and a fluttering heartbeat.

Fiona realized she should probably stop staring at him as if he'd grown a third eye. Moving a few feet down the bar, she pretended to straighten glasses that didn't need straightening, sending subtle glances in his direction now and again. He swiveled around on the stool, one arm resting on the bar, his large hand wrapped around the mug as he focused on the television suspended in the corner above the pool table.

How silly that she should be having such a strong reaction to this guy. His gold loop earrings, one in each lobe, and collar-length dark hair hanging down from beneath the cap made him seem just a little bit too dangerous. Of course, she hadn't been involved with anyone since the breakup with her erstwhile fiancé, Paul the potato farmer. Unfortunately, for the past few years, she'd been in a man famine. But Paul hadn't been the adventurous sort, and he hadn't given any credence to Fiona's dreams of owning and managing her own hotel. He'd simply told her goodbye when she'd asked him to come with her. Granted, that farewell had stung like a hornet, but now that she'd had some distance, she realized that she wasn't suited for a man like Paul. He'd preferred the quiet life and crops; she preferred bright lights and big city—and craved adventure.

Adventure was sitting only a few feet away in the form of a demigod with a black clothing fetish. A man who could probably show her the time of her life, if she worked up enough nerve to make the suggestion.

Fiona mentally cataloged all the bad pickup lines she'd experienced in her twenty-five years. Mind if I suck your lips off your face? Too obvious. Could I show you the back seat of my sedan? Too Benny Jack. Besides, her car was temporarily out of commission. And apparently so were her seduction skills.

Come-ons were not her forte, but she decided it was now or never. She would engage him in a conversation. Something simple. The weather. Jockeys or briefs?

Inhaling a cleansing breath, Fiona grabbed a moderately clean rag and began working her way back in his direction. When she was only inches from his hand, she asked, ''Would you like more coffee?''

''Not presently.'' He subtly surveyed the area, something that might be lost on any casual observer, but not on Fiona.

''Are you looking for someone?'' she asked.

He shifted back around to face her. ''Yes.''

A man of few words. But that would not deter her. Tonight she would become Fiona the Fearless Flirt. ''A woman?''

''No.''

Fiona wanted to cheer. ''Okay. What does your friend look like? Maybe I've seen him around.''

''He is definitely not a friend.''

From his acid tone, Fiona wondered if she would soon have a fight on her hands. ''I'm guessing he's an enemy, right?''

He gave her a questioning look. ''Are you interested in astrology?''

A totally unexpected question. Fiona didn't see him as an astrology kind of guy, and frankly she was hard-pressed to believe that planet alignment controlled fate. Where was the tall dark stranger who was supposed to enter her life when Mars was in retro-something? Sitting right in front of her.

What the heck. She'd play along. ''I find astrology somewhat intriguing. In fact, I'd bet you're a Scorpio.'' The oversexed sign.

''Correct.''

Bingo! Darn, Fiona, you're good.

His eyes narrowed. ''Are you a Leo?''

No, she was a Pisces. But if he wanted her to be a Leo, she could do that. She liked lions. In fact, he made her want to growl. "How'd you guess?"

He hesitated a moment then said, "I did not realize you were a woman."

Ouch. Did she look that awful? And did he think she had bowling balls stuffed in her shirt? Granted, she'd always considered being a bit top heavy somewhat of a curse for someone with such a small frame, yet she'd never expected anyone to believe they weren't real, or that she was a cross dresser. But, after all, this *was* Vegas. And it would be just her luck if he was gay. "Yes, I'm a woman. If you want a drag club, you might try downtown or the Strip."

"My apologies." His gaze settled on her breasts. "It is quite obvious you're a woman. I meant I was not informed of your gender."

Okay, she could forgive him. But she was still a trifle confused and a whole lot warm when he leaned forward and asked, "Have you seen anything?"

She saw the crease framing the right of his mouth that probably turned into a dimple when he smiled, something he had yet to do. But Fiona smiled, a coy one, or at least she hoped it looked flirtatious and not forced. "I've seen just about everything. What exactly are you looking for?"

Before he could answer, the drunk Fiona had ousted not more than hour ago picked that inopportune time to burst through the door, clamoring for a beer.

Fiona pushed back from the bar and said, "You don't need to be in here, Chuck. I'm not going to serve you."

Ignoring Fiona, Chuck staggered behind the bar. "Just one more brewsky."

Fiona scowled at him and pointed at the door. "You've had enough, now leave."

"Aw, come on, Fee-Fee."

He was pushing his luck now. "Go home, Chuck."

"After you give me another drink," he slurred, bringing

his foul breath with him as he leaned forward and pointed a bratwurst finger in her face.

"Do what the lady asks or you will have to answer to me."

Fiona glanced at Scorpio who now stood by the stool, looking and sounding like a dark knight bent on coming to her rescue. And they'd said chivalry was passé. What did they know? Regardless, even if she didn't have a black belt in karate, or any color of belt for that matter, she was quite capable of taking care of herself. "He's harmless," she assured him before regarding the drunk again.

When Chuck clutched Fiona's collar in both beefy fists, Fiona grabbed his wrists and shouted, "Back off!" thrusting her knee upward toward the intended target, but Chuck moved back before she could do any damage. No, not moved back. Yanked back by Scorpio who had somehow scaled the bar and now had the drunk pinned against the counter. He muttered something in a language that Fiona couldn't understand, but she didn't think he was telling Chuckie to have a nice night.

He shot a glance at Fiona. "What do you wish me to do with him?"

"Just put him out the door. I'll call the police if he comes back in."

Chuck looked as if he might blubber as Scorpio grabbed him by the nape and guided him toward the exit. Fiona felt like blubbering, too, as she watched her one opportunity to have some adventure walk out the door, probably never to return.

Darn. Another night in Dullsville.

As Darin stepped into the warm night, he silently cursed the drunk, cursed the fact that he'd been caught off guard by the FBI operative's gender. He'd expected a man when Kent had told him the agent would operate under the code name Leo, not an attractive woman with hair the color of a sunset, large green eyes and perfect breasts that he had not been able to ignore. But he must ignore her if he intended to complete his mission. He had no time for a liaison or lover even if he'd entertained those thoughts when he had first set eyes on her. That was before he realized she would serve as his partner in apprehending Birkenfeld, not his partner beneath tangled sheets.

As soon as he deposited the drunk in the parking lot, he would return inside to the agent and discuss their plans before Birkenfeld's scheduled arrival in one hour. He would also attempt to keep his eyes off her attributes, though that might prove difficult. But if all went well tonight, Darin would be back on the plane tomorrow morning and Birkenfeld would be back behind bars. And he would leave the woman behind without discovering if the fiery passion she seemed to possess held true in bed. Under different circumstances, he might attempt to find out.

Darin guided Chuck down the steps while the drunk whined, "Don't hurt me, man."

He had no intention of hurting him unless he attempted to harm the agent, although he suspected the woman could handle this troublemaker. After all, she had been trained by the best.

As they reached the walkway at the bottom of the steps, a passing man with a shaved head, his eyes lowered to the ground, muttered, "Excuse me."

Darin's blood ran cold at the sound of the voice.

With one hand on the drunk's neck, the other poised on the gun beneath his jacket, Darin turned and said, "Roman Birkenfeld."

The man spun around and their gazes connected. Recognition dawned in the demonic doctor's beady eyes before he shoved Chuck into Darin and took off.

Pushing the drunk aside, Darin gave chase, adrenaline pumping through his veins, his heart pounding with every step as he closed in on the criminal, but not before Birkenfeld disappeared around the back of the building.

Flattening himself against the brick wall, Darin moved into the dimly lit alley, his gun drawn, and came upon two figures struggling on the ground. He saw the shock of red hair then the silver glint of a knife poised above the woman's chest as she fought to hold Birkenfeld's arm at bay, shouting, "Get off me, you jackass!" Memories of another place, another time, another woman assaulted him.

Sheer instinct drove him forward to grab Birkenfeld by the arm. In a split second of stupidity, Darin took his attention from the fugitive in order to make certain the woman was not injured, allowing Birkenfeld the opportunity to strike.

The knife hit home, slashing first across Darin's left thigh, then his side. Anger overrode the pain but he couldn't see well enough to take a clean shot without risking shooting the agent who'd entered the fray, pummeling the back of Birkenfeld's neck but doing little to hinder the criminal's knife-wielding. Darin kicked out, landing the toe of his boot in Birkenfeld's ribs, and at the same time the blade cut across the back of his right ankle. The blow proved to be too much, dropping Darin to the gravel surface. The gun, wrenched from his grasp at the impact, skittered across the pitted pavement, leaving them both vulnerable.

Darin heard the sound of harried footsteps and rolled to his belly, fumbling for and finding the gun, but not soon enough to prevent Birkenfeld from escaping into the night before he could fire off a round.

He eased onto his back, his chest heaving from labored breaths, his head swimming from the wounds and the tactical errors he had committed. The mistakes of his past seemed bent on recurring whenever a woman's safety was involved.

Turning his head to his right, he found the agent on her knees next to him. At least she was alive. "Are you hurt?" he managed.

"I'm fine." She gave him a visual once-over, pausing at his thigh. "Oh, God, you're bleeding!"

Darin worked his way into a sitting position to assess the damage. The guard light above them provided enough illumination to see the slit in the T-shirt on his right side below his ribs. Fortunately, the jacket had provided enough protection against severe damage to his flesh. His thigh injury was worse, a dark stain fanning from the perimeter of the gash in his pants, indicating blood. But his ankle ached more and he suspected Birkenfeld's knife had done the most damage there. Nothing that would not heal, but it would hinder his pursuit, at least tonight.

He muttered several oaths in Arabic directed at his carelessness.

"I'll call an ambulance," the agent said, her voice surprisingly calm.

Darin clasped her wrist before she could stand. "No hospitals. No doctors."

Her eyes widened. "Are you nuts?"

"I've had worse injury, I assure you. Did you not have your gun drawn when you encountered Birkenfeld?"

"Birkenfeld?"

Obviously she was somewhat in shock. "The fugitive whom you were engaging in hand-to-hand combat."

She frowned. "First, I don't own a gun. Second, he ran into me when I was coming out the back with the garbage. Third, I don't know any Birkenfeld."

Darin scowled. "Did they not inform you that he was the man we would be apprehending?"

"Who are they? And who are you?"

Darin suddenly realized he had made two grave errors. "You are not FBI?"

She attempted a weak smile. "You have the F and B right, but that would be for Fiona the Bartender."

He gritted his teeth, braced his elbows on bent knees and lowered his head. Ben had been correct in assuming he was not the right man for this mission. Yet, now more than ever, Darin wanted Birkenfeld to pay.

She came to her feet and wiped her hands over her jean-covered thighs. "Let me get the bartender who just came in to relieve me. He can help me get you inside."

"No."

"Why not?"

Because the bartender was more than likely the real FBI agent, and Darin did not want the man to know what a fool he'd been. Letting Birkenfeld escape had been Darin's mistake, and he would correct it. But how? He was injured. He could not do this alone. He would need help, something he hated to admit.

Darin leveled his gaze on Fiona, her expression a mixture of confusion and concern. Even if she was not FBI, she was his only ally at the moment. He would be forced to rely on her assistance, if she was willing to give it. "Do you live nearby?"

"I have an apartment a couple of miles away."

"Take me there."

She braced her hands on her waist and stared down on him. "First, you have to tell me who you are and what this is all about."

He would only tell her what he must to reassure her. He would not subject her to more danger by revealing everything. "If you will see me to your apartment, I will give you details. I will say that I am working for law enforcement. The man named Birkenfeld is very dangerous. I'm here to apprehend him."

Fiona's expression brightened. "So you're one of the good guys?"

"Yes."

She frowned. "How do I know that?"

Darin lifted his arms from his sides. "In the right pocket of my pants, you will find my credentials."

She crouched down and rifled in his pocket for a few moments. Had he not been in such pain, he might have enjoyed the activity. After she withdrew the black folder, she looked at the fabricated license, looked back at him, then back at the license. "Frank Scorpio? Texas Peace Officer?"

"That is correct." He shifted his leg and winced from the pain in his ankle. "Could we possibly leave soon?"

"I have to call a cab. My car's in the shop."

"I have a rental in the lot."

"Okay, but I'm driving." She rose to her feet again. "I'll have the new guy lock up. It'll only take a sec, so don't go anywhere."

"I promise I will be here when you return. And do not tell him I am here. The fewer people who know, the better."

"Okay." She pointed to the gun still in his grip. "Could you put that thing away? It makes me nervous."

Darin holstered the Beretta for now, but he would take it out again in case Birkenfeld returned. "Anything else I might do for you before I bleed to death?"

She gave him a self-conscious smile. "I'll hurry."

Fiona sprinted back into the building, leaving Darin alone in the alley with his pain and the strong sense that getting involved with this woman could be the third mistake he'd made since his arrival in Vegas.

But he had no choice.

Roman Birkenfeld ran into the night. Ran until his lungs burned and his eyes teared. Ran aimlessly through the darkened streets. His throbbing side slowed his progress somewhat and he paused behind an odious commercial trash bin to feel along his ribs where Shakir had kicked him. Nothing broken, only bruised, he suspected. No punctured lung, otherwise he wouldn't be able to breathe at all.

Damn the woman who'd run into him. He should've killed her. He would have, had it not been for that bastard, Shakir. The recollection of his knife slicing through the man's skin gave him added strength and a good deal of purpose as he continued on at a sprint. He didn't have to guess how Shakir had found him. The idiot Larry Sutter. The blood-sucking attorney had no doubt ratted him out, setting him up with a promise of money, enough money to purchase passage out of the country. He should have known not to trust him. Should have known that Sutter had lied when he'd said he was leaving the hospital, the meeting tonight a ruse to protect Sutter's ass.

Damn Shakir and Sutter. If Shakir wasn't dead, and he

hoped he was, he would find a way to take him out. He would take them both out, beginning with Sutter. But how? He couldn't get close to the hospital; they would recognize him.

Tommy Stokes. The ex-con had escaped from Texas but no doubt he would be back in Vegas by now, frequenting his favorite haunts, keeping company with less-than-upstanding citizens. Places where anyone could get anything, if the price was right. Business was good for a man with a thirst for blood and the absence of a soul.

He didn't have money to pay Stokes, but one thing was working in his favor—the thug hated lawyers. Stokes would agree to off Sutter for the sheer pleasure of watching him suffer as payback for the attorney who hadn't saved him from a five-year prison term. Now he would just have to find the ex-con, and he would. Tonight.

As it had been all of Roman Birkenfeld's life, people had tried to thwart his goals. They hadn't succeeded until now. His medical career was a bust, all the years of hard work and struggle gone down the tubes because of some determined East Coast loan sharks and a woman who'd enlisted a group of Texas vigilantes determined to destroy him. It always came back to a woman, in this case, Natalie Perez.

Natalie was out of reach this time, but Shakir wasn't. Someone would have to pay. It might as well be him.

Two

Fiona had finally composed herself enough on the drive to the apartment to stop shaking and help Frank out of the car. Well, she'd wanted some adventure, and she'd definitely gotten it when she'd been rescued from a crazed criminal by a dark stranger with biceps bulging from his iron-man arm now thrown over her shoulder. Thank goodness she lived on the first floor of the complex. No way would she have been able to drag him up the stairs. At least she was still in one piece, thanks to him. If he hadn't come along, the guy might have killed her. But she sure as heck hadn't intended to give up without a fight, especially when he'd held her down. Fiona could not tolerate being held down, and that had been more frightening than his knife.

After leaning her savior against the wall outside her apartment, she said, "Hang on a sec," then turned the lock, pushed open the door and was immediately greeted by Carlotta, her slobbering, over-fed, Shar Pei who possessed enough wrinkles to keep spray starch in business for years. She stopped long enough to pat the dog's tan head and ask, "Hey, Lottie, what did you destroy today?" The answer to the question came in the form of random scraps that had once been a textbook scattered in the corner on the living room floor.

Fiona pointed a finger at the guilty hound. "Bad, bad girl." As usual, Lottie responded to the scolding by feigning innocence.

Taking Lottie by the collar, Fiona guided her into the lone bedroom and closed the door on her mournful expression before going back to Frank.

Frank. Ha! That just didn't fit. In fact, she hadn't bought that bogus name any more than she was buying his story about being a Texas cop. But she really hoped he was a member of some law enforcement agency and not some drug dealer from the back side of the law. She'd already taken a huge risk by not taking him to the hospital. And she'd be taking a bigger one if she allowed him in the apartment. But she couldn't in good conscience leave him bleeding on her doorstep. He was hurt and he needed her help. Maybe she might even earn some commendation for valor. Just getting a good look at him in the light would be enough reward.

On that thought she turned around to find he'd already made himself welcome on her green chintz sofa, his long legs stretched out in front of him, head tipped back against the cushions, his dark lashes fanning out below his closed eyes. The man was just too gorgeous for his own good. He also looked a little pasty, and she worried he'd passed out from the loss of blood. If that proved to be the case, she was calling 911 whether he wanted that or not.

Fiona closed the front door and double locked it in case the creepy criminal had followed them. Or had she locked herself in with a criminal?

Fiona, you are a fool. But she had to trust her instincts and her belief that she was safe with her friend, Frank.

She stood over him, her gaze coming to rest on the gash at his thigh where she'd fashioned a tourniquet with two bar towels, there and around his ankle. She took a seat next to him to get a closer look at his injured side, pulling back the jacket a bit to find the bleeding had been minimal. She couldn't be sure about his thigh unless he took off his pants. Considering they'd only met a few hours ago, disrobing him didn't seem at all appropriate. But it was pretty darned tempting.

Slowly Fiona lowered her hand toward his fly then drew back. She couldn't do it, but she could take a peek at the cut by removing the towel, or at least until she had permission to take off his clothes. His pants, she corrected. Only his pants and only to administer some first aid.

As she gingerly gripped the knotted towel with her fingertips, his large hand clamped her wrist with the speed of a cobra, causing her to nearly jump out of her own skin or at the very least, off the sofa.

"What are you doing?" he asked without opening his eyes or releasing her wrist.

At least he wasn't comatose. "I'm trying to look at your wound. It needs to be cleaned up."

He raised his head and stared at her with those intense black eyes that made her want to squirm and sweat. "Do you have any antiseptic?"

"You're in luck. I have that and some bandages." And limited first aid knowledge thanks to her one-year stint as a volunteer member of Shadowvale, Idaho's, fire and rescue unit. Of course, she'd probably been on three whole calls during that time, none that had involved knife wounds. "I'll do what I can, but I'm not making any guarantees."

"I would appreciate any assistance you might give me." He gave her a look of concern. "Are you certain you're not injured?"

She was moved by the sincerity in his expression and his worry over her well-being. At least he had that much honor. "I promise, I'm fine. Nothing more than a scratch or two on my back."

"I'm relieved. I was afraid he might have cut you, as well."

"He tried, but I managed to keep him from doing it."

"Unfortunately, I cannot say the same for myself."

"But you saved me. I doubt we'd be here now if you hadn't come along."

"Had it not been for me, you would not have been put in that position."

Fiona didn't care to debate the workings of fate, so she said, "Uh, you might want to get comfortable. I mean, you might need to take off..." Why couldn't she just say it?

He lifted a dark brow. "My pants?"

"Yeah. So I can see it better. Your cut. The one on your thigh. And your boots and socks, of course."

"Should I remove my shirt, as well?" He sounded almost amused, but then she sounded like a blithering idiot.

Her traitorous gaze picked that moment to land on his fly. "Sure. Or I could just lift it up." She yanked her attention back to his face. "Your shirt, I mean."

For a minute she thought he might actually smile, but it didn't happen. "Anything else you require of me?"

"Can I have my hand back now?" she asked.

"Most certainly," he said as he released his grip, but not before he brushed the inside of her wrist with a fingertip. Or at least that's what she thought he'd done. Maybe she was just hovering in imagination overdrive.

Attacked by a sudden case of the chills, Fiona came to her feet and pulled the throw her grandmother had knitted from the back of the chair. It was lopsided and an interesting shade of lime green, but it should be big enough to provide some privacy for him should he decide to undress. Of course, there was the matter of all those little holes and loose threads, thanks to Lottie's incessant chewing. But it was the best she could do at the moment.

She tossed him the throw and told him, "You can cover up with this," then headed for the bathroom before she did something really stupid—like insist he remove his pants immediately so she could get a good look at all his assets. How desperate she must be to consider seducing an injured stranger. At least she'd be assured he wouldn't be able to move very fast.

Stop it, Fiona.

Once in the bathroom, she rummaged through the cabinet beneath the sink, knocking over several boxes and bottles before she found what she needed. After retrieving bandages, a damp rag and some antiseptic cream, she made her way back into the living room…and nearly dropped the supplies she clutched tightly to her chest.

Two bare, blatantly masculine legs covered in a fine layer of dark hair extended from their owner who had stretched out on his back lengthwise, his head resting on the sofa's arm and his eyes once again closed against the light. His bare chest, smooth as a baby's behind except for a slight shading of hair between his pecs, revealed valleys and planes of tanned muscular terrain. No shoes, no socks, no denying the man was prime perfection without his clothes. But Fiona couldn't see anything vital due to the throw draped across his manly strategic area.

Manly strategic area? A few hours in his presence and she was thinking in sexual military-speak. She was also thinking that she would bet her dog that he had one notable missile beneath his briefs. Black briefs, she'd guess. Maybe she would have the opportunity to confirm that. And she needed to get her mind out of the sewer and back on the situation at hand—examining his wounds, not his essentials.

Fiona dropped to her knees beside the sofa and considered praying to Planet Mars for strength. Instead, she took the warm cloth and pressed it against his side. His eyes drifted open but she saw no indication she was hurting him.

She focused on the cut, willing her hand to hold steady. "This doesn't look too bad. I don't think it even needs a bandage." She could use one to tape her mouth closed before she moaned with approval.

"Only a scratch," he said, his voice grainy and seriously sensual. "I'm more concerned with my thigh and ankle."

Fiona was more concerned with what was above his thigh.

Putting away those concerns for the time being, she scooted down and examined the gash. "This looks worse. It could probably use a few stitches."

"A bandage will suffice."

"If you say so," she said as she dabbed at the cut, then applied the ointment. After positioning several adhesive glow-in-the-dark, happy-face bandages lengthwise across his skin, she noticed they did little to close the edges of the wound. But boy, did he have one heck of a solid thigh. Lots of muscle and tone. She wondered if he did squats or if he just came by his physique naturally.

He scrutinized the bandages, looking displeased. "Very festive. And somewhat ridiculous."

"It's all I have, so you'll have to live with it."

"My ankle now," he said in a tone that sounded just a little too demanding.

She sent him an acid look. "I'm getting to that. Roll over."

He did, and Fiona nearly swallowed her razor-sharp tongue. Well, now she knew. He didn't have on black briefs or white ones. He didn't have on boxers, either. Nothing covered his sculpted buttocks aside from taut skin a shade paler than his hair-spattered thighs. His lack of underwear somewhat surprised her, not to mention what it did to unseen places on her person. She could analyze his reason for removing his drawers, or she could get back down to business and check out his ankle.

But who in their right mind wanted to look at a foot when faced with a fine, bare bottom? Come to think of it, she had no doubt his feet were probably as sexy as the rest of him.

Fiona tore her gaze away from his fanny and forced her attention on his injured ankle. When she flexed his foot forward, revealing the depth of the gash, she heard his sharp intake of breath, the only indication whatsoever he was in any pain.

This particular wound was much worse than the others. This cut couldn't be fixed right with a few flimsy bandages and cream. Since he had his face now buried in his folded arms, Fiona stared at his bare back that sported a lengthy horizontal scar. "You need to go to the hospital."

"It will heal."

"Dear Frank," she said in a syrupy-sweet voice. "The guy nearly cut your foot off. You'll be lucky if you're able to walk on it again. Someone needs to look at this."

He regarded her over one broad shoulder. "Do you know a doctor? Someone you can trust?"

Fiona didn't know any doctors aside from the one she'd seen annually since she'd been in Vegas. She doubted he made house calls, and even if he did, this was not a gynecological problem. But she did know Peg, her friend two doors down who worked as a nurse in a medical office. Peg might know what to do. It was worth a shot.

Fiona pushed up from the floor to stand. "I know a woman who can help."

He frowned. "A female doctor?"

"Do you have something against women, Frankie?"

He looked as if he'd just downed a dill pickle. "No, and I do not answer to Frankie."

"Your name's not Frank at all, is it?"

"No."

"Then do you mind telling me your real name? I mean, you're naked on my sofa so I think we should be on a first-name basis, don't you?"

"You may call me Scorpio."

Drat him. "Okay, you may call me Fiona. And if you call me Fee-Fee or Red, I will pour salt in your wounds, is that understood?"

A smile curved his full lips, bringing the dimple and perfect white teeth into view. "Are you always this aggressive?"

"Honey, you don't know the half of it." But he would.

With that, she left behind his sinful grin and beautiful butt to make the call to Peg in the kitchen. But she couldn't escape the vision of him lying on her couch—or the one of him lying in her bed, naked, taking her on an all-night journey to cloud nine. As if *that* was going to happen.

* * *

Darin had believed knife wounds would serve as a deterrent to a man's desire. He'd been wrong. When Fiona had touched his side, he'd experienced the first sexual stirrings. When she'd moved to his thigh, he'd grown as hard as his handgun. Of course, when she'd manipulated his injured foot, that had somewhat alleviated any thoughts of sex. But even now, even though his ankle still throbbed, he would gladly relieve his current predicament in her bed, deep inside her body, in order to keep his mind off his injuries, and his errors.

Working his way back into a sitting position, he left the ugly blanket draped across his lap to hide the effect of his questionable cravings, urges most likely resulting from adrenaline and the length of time since he'd been to bed with a woman. He had no cause to consider seduction when his mission was paramount. It would be best to allow Fiona's medical friend to treat the wounds, then be on his way.

"She's on her way," Fiona said as she reentered the room and took the very pink chair across from him.

"Good. And she is a physician?"

"She's a part-time nurse."

"This is your idea of medical expertise?"

She folded her arms beneath her breasts. "Do you have any better ideas?"

Yes, he did, but they had nothing to do with tending his injuries and everything to do with learning each curve, each crevice of her enticing body with his hands and mouth. He moved his injured foot, sending a sharp pain up the back of his leg in order to limit his increasing erection, and to remind him of his goals. "I would appreciate any medical attention she can provide. And if you will retrieve my bag from the trunk of the car, I will have clothes available for my departure."

She brought her legs onto the cushions and crossed them in front of her. "You really don't think you're going anywhere tonight, do you?"

"I must if I wish to continue my mission."

"You're going to go running through the back alleys of Vegas looking for this Birkenfeld who has—" she checked her watch "—about an hour's head start? Do you plan to do that on your knees?"

He could certainly think of one thing he would like to do on his knees before her. "I have endured worse injury." To his body. To his soul.

She sent him a skeptical look. "I'm sure you have. But even if you do manage to walk out of here, and I have my doubts you can tonight, don't you think he's probably long gone by now, maybe even left the state?"

"Not likely."

"How do you know for sure?"

She asked too many questions, required too many answers, knew too much already. But Darin had possibly put her in peril by having her bring him here. The least he could do was reveal a few details. Perhaps then she would understand the consequences if Birkenfeld was not captured immediately. "Can I trust that whatever I tell you will go no further?"

"My lips are sealed and I'm all ears."

She was all sensual, seductive woman, Darin decided before forcing his thoughts back to the dire situation at hand. "Birkenfeld established a black-market adoption ring he operated using his obstetrics practice as a front. He stole newborns and sold them for large amounts of money. He also murdered a doctor in Texas in order to assume his identity so he could infiltrate a hospital, looking for a woman whose infant he had attempted to kidnap. Fortunately, he was stopped before he could harm her but later escaped authorities."

"He's a murderer and a baby thief?" Anger resonated in her tone, the same anger Darin had experienced each time he considered Birkenfeld's crimes.

"He needs money to pay off East Coast loan sharks and to feed his gambling habit," he continued. "We have an informant who claims that Birkenfeld has connections here that will enable him to obtain funds. This city also has places where he can easily hide." But Darin would ferret him out, and soon. Birkenfeld would not escape again.

She remained silent for a few moments as if needing time to analyze the information. "Look, even if that's true and he's still in town, you can't accomplish anything tonight with a bum ankle, especially if you're not sure where to look."

She had a valid point, though Darin was reluctant to admit it. "I suppose you're correct in terms of Birkenfeld going underground."

"Of course I am. You can stay here tonight then go after him again in the morning, if you're feeling up to the challenge."

When she streaked her tongue over her bottom lip, Darin recognized he was definitely *up* for one challenge unrelated to Birkenfeld.

A strange shuffling sound drew his attention from Fiona's mouth to the closed door adjacent to the living area. "What is that noise?"

She lifted one shoulder in a shrug. "It's just Lottie. She heard I had a naked man on the couch."

This was all Darin needed, involving another innocent party. "You should have informed me we are not alone."

"Oh, you can trust her. She won't say a word. I'd let her out but she'd just jump all over you and lick your face."

Hearing the word *lick* did nothing to help Darin's threatening state of arousal. "Does she always greet your guests in that manner?"

"Oh, yeah. She's kind of wild." Fiona nodded toward the shreds of paper strewn across the floor in the corner. "Today she got bored and tore up my textbook."

"Are you a student?"

"College student. I'm studying hotel management. And in case you haven't guessed, Lottie is my dog."

He was relieved over both revelations. Being alone in an apartment with a woman not of legal age would be another mistake in a long line of many. "I had assumed you were older."

Her smile faded. "Gee, thanks."

He was failing miserably at all his endeavors tonight, but at least he had kept her alive. "I meant older than your early twenties."

"I'm twenty-five, almost twenty-six. I started my career late. Better late than never, I guess."

"Are you from Las Vegas?"

"Actually, I'm from Idaho. I've been here for a few years. I work the bar at night to pay for my school and this dump."

Darin could not fathom being without adequate funds. He admired her conviction as much as he admired her body. However, he did find her stubborn nature somewhat disconcerting on one level. On another, he found it intriguing. That much passion might translate well in bed. He shifted and looked away.

"How about you?" she asked, again drawing his attention. "Have you always lived in Texas?"

"I have lived everywhere. I have no permanent home."

"Everyone has to start out somewhere, Scorpio," she said. "My guess is that you're not originally from the States."

"Your guess is correct. I was born in a small country near Oman, but I have not been back for some time."

"No wife or girlfriend waiting for you? Or are you the kind of guy who has a girl at every stop?"

"I have no ties." He wanted no ties.

"What about your parents?"

"Both dead."

She looked sympathetic. "I'm sorry. My dad died when I was young, but my mom's still alive. She taught me everything I know about bartending because that's how she supported us. She makes the best gin martini in the good old U. S. of A. Probably in the world. She also taught me how to fight when the situation called for it."

Her ability to fight had been apparent to Darin when she'd taken on Birkenfeld in the alley. At least he was somewhat assured she could handle herself during a dangerous situation—but only to a point. He would make certain she was not faced with that prospect again—all the more reason for him to make a quick exit from the apartment and her life.

A bark and a whine came from the room at the same time the knock sounded, saving Darin from having to answer questions of a personal nature. He had already revealed more to her than he should.

When he started to stand, she pointed a finger at him and said, "Don't get up. It's just Peg."

"Make certain before you open the door," Darin cautioned. "Birkenfeld could have followed us."

She frowned. "And I'm so sure he would be polite enough to knock before he kicked down the door."

When Fiona walked to the entry, Darin withdrew his gun from the discarded holster on the table and laid it on his lap. He, too, greatly doubted that Birkenfeld would knock, but he intended to be prepared for anything, although he had not been prepared for this woman named Fiona.

He questioned his wisdom in spending the night with her—a woman who had sparked his imagination and effectively lowered his guard, something that could prove costly if he did not practice more care. Yet the prospect of giving her one night of pleasure beyond the limits caused his body to stir to life once more. He was in no shape to chase after Birkenfeld tonight, but he wasn't totally incapacitated. Despite his caution and his wounds, he would most gladly make love to her in ways she would not soon forget.

But only if she agreed to the terms. No ties. No emotional entanglement. No promises. Whatever happened between them during those hours between dark and dawn would be solely up to her.

Tomorrow he would return to his solitary existence where nothing mattered beyond the mission. He had no need for a permanent relationship—even though at times he longed for that very thing.

Fiona peeked through the peephole to see fifty-something Peg standing on the threshold dressed in baggy red-heart-spattered white pajamas, her brown hair shooting from her scalp like frizzy fireworks. "It's her," she told Scorpio without turning around.

She opened the door only far enough so she could slip outside to join her neighbor on the porch, closing the door behind her. "That was fast."

Peg held up a brown bag. "This is what I had on hand. A few butterfly closures, gauze wrap and tape and some antibiotic samples. I wasn't about to go traipsing down to the clinic this time of night and risk setting off the alarm."

Fiona took the bag and looked inside. "Thanks, Peg. You're a jewel, as always."

"So where is it?" Peg asked.

"Where is what?"

"Your cut?"

"I don't have a cut."

She nodded toward the bag clutched in Fiona's hand. "Then who is that for?"

"A friend."

Peg frowned. "A friend? Fiona, you better hope your 'friend' isn't allergic to penicillin. I don't want to be responsible if they go into anaphylactic shock. I could lose my job."

"I'll be sure to ask him."

Peg's wide smile farther inflated her dumpling cheeks. "Him? You got a man in there?"

Boy, Fiona had really done it now. "Yes, and don't start making assumptions."

Before Fiona could issue a protest, Peg stepped to one side on the porch and peered into the picture window through the break in the curtains. Her mouth dropped open and her eyes went wide. "You have a half-naked man with a gun on your couch!"

"He has his gun out?" Fiona moved behind Peg to confirm that fact.

Peg turned, alarm in her blue eyes. "Is he holding you hostage?"

In a manner of speaking, at least her libido. "Of course

not. I would've called the police. In fact, he is the police, working undercover.'' And she could imagine how well he would work under the covers. ''That's why he has the gun. He got into a fight at the bar and he doesn't want to blow his cover by going to a hospital.''

Peg turned back to the window. ''Impressive gun. Impressive guy. How well does his other pistol work?''

Fiona took Peg's pudgy arm and pulled her back around and away from the window. ''This is not what you think, Peg.'' Unfortunately.

Peg smirked. ''Are you sure the sex didn't get a little wild and you clawed him?''

''In my dreams.''

''Well, if I were you, I'd make those dreams a reality. You're already halfway there. You got him naked.''

''He got himself naked.''

Peg shrugged. ''A minor point. Now all you have to do is get yourself naked and climb onboard the temptation train.''

''Don't be obtuse, Peg. He's beat-up. He's not interested in sex.''

Peg released a metal-scraping laugh. ''And don't be stupid, Fiona. I don't know one man who would let a little cut stop him from having sex.''

''It's not a little cut, Peg. It's three cuts, and one's pretty bad. That's why I need you to take a look, as long as you promise not to ask any questions.''

''I promise.''

''And no snide remarks.''

''I'll try,'' she said with less conviction.

Fiona opened the door and Peg followed close behind her. Scorpio was still sitting on the couch, the throw now wrapped around his waist. Fortunately, he'd put the gun back in its holster.

Fiona gestured at Peg and said, ''Frank, this is my neighbor, Peggy Jones. She's going to see what she can do about your cuts.''

Scorpio nodded at Peg. ''I would be grateful for your aid.''

Peg elbowed Fiona aside and plopped her hefty frame next to Scorpio. "No problem. Now show me where it hurts."

He lifted the throw, exposing his thigh to Peg's scrutiny. "This isn't going to do," she said, and began ripping away the bandages. Fiona figured the poor guy's thighs would be stripped of hair before Peg was done with him, yet Scorpio's expression remained impassive. Obviously, he had a high pain threshold.

After Peg closed the wound with the sturdier strips she'd brought with her, she said, "Okay, that's one down, two to go. Where are the others?"

"The cut on his side isn't that bad," Fiona said. "He has to turn over for you to see the worst one." She immediately regretted her words when Peg sent her a devilish look. "It's on his ankle."

Peg stood. "Okay, Frank. Roll over and let me see."

After Scorpio complied, again burying his face on his folded arms, Peg sat down on the sofa and rested his foot in her lap. The look she sent Fiona this time was void of humor and full of concern. "This is pretty nasty. I'm not sure the strips are going to hold it all that well. I wouldn't be surprised if you've nicked a tendon."

Scorpio glanced back at her. "Do what you can. I will manage."

"You might manage to get one hell of an infection," Peg said. "But you don't need to walk on it for at least two days, if you live that long."

Scorpio's face showed no sign of fear. "I assure you I will live."

"He's had worse injuries," Fiona added, apparent from the jagged scar on his back.

Peg sealed the slash the same way she had his thigh, then wrapped it tightly in gauze. After she was finished, she patted the back of his calf as if he were a child. "Okay, sugar. We're all done here. Don't blame me when you get gangrene." She stood and stared down on him. "Are you allergic to penicillin?"

Scorpio resumed a sitting position, careful to keep the throw bound around his waist. "I have no allergies."

"Good." She dug in the bag and handed Fiona the box of samples. "Give him two of these a day for seven days. If he spikes a temp, get him to the hospital."

"I'll try." Fiona figured she would probably have to call in the cavalry to convince Scorpio to cooperate. Besides, she doubted he'd be around for more than one day, much less seven.

"I am grateful for your assistance, Ms. Jones," Scorpio said.

Peg sent him a sunny smile. "Oh, you're welcome. My husband and I would love to have you and Fiona over for dinner."

"He's leaving soon," Fiona added before Peg had the opportunity to suggest she help pick out the wedding cake. "Isn't Walt waiting for you?"

Peg kept her gaze locked on Scorpio, laid a palm over her liberal chest and giggled like a schoolgirl. "Walt's my husband."

Scorpio's smile seemed strained but sincere. "He is a very lucky man."

Oh, brother, Fiona thought as she took Peg's arm, turned her toward the door and guided her outside. She pulled the door closed when Peg kept trying to look inside. "Thanks bunches, neighbor. I owe you a lot for this."

Peg patted Fiona's cheek. "Yes, you do, sugar. And you owe yourself to get to know that one a whole lot better. He is one fine specimen."

Fiona couldn't agree more. "He's a friend, Peg. Just a friend."

"Sure, Fiona. And I'm too old to have sex." Peg glanced in the direction of her apartment. "Which reminds me. I left Walt in bed and almost in the mood. If I hurry, maybe he won't be in REM sleep yet. If he gets that far, I can forget about getting some action."

Wonderful. Peg and Walt, and probably Benny Jack and

his date, were all going to have sex, and Fiona was having a hard time getting Scorpio to smile at her. "By all means, go and rouse Walt."

"Okey-dokey. And you go and rouse the hunk."

Peg pivoted on her furry pink slippers and headed down the walkway while Fiona pushed back into the apartment, closing and locking the door behind her.

"I'll be back in a minute." She bypassed Scorpio and went into the kitchen to draw a glass of water so he could wash down the antibiotics. On afterthought, she retrieved a bottle of pills she'd had filled following a little incident in the bar where she'd intervened in a brawl between two regulars. Who would have thought that a seventy-year-old senior would have packed such a powerful right hook? Fiona's jaw had learned that lesson the hard way.

The bottle was almost full since she'd only taken one of the painkillers that had basically rendered her brainless. Scorpio would need something for pain in order to sleep, whether he cared to admit it or not. She shook one pill from the bottle as directed, then took out one more. Considering his size, he probably needed two to garner any relief.

Fiona strode back into the living room and offered him the glass of water and the pills housed in her open palm. "Here. These will make you feel better."

He eyed the capsules with disdain. "I do not see the necessity."

"Well, I do. One will thwart infection, the other two are for pain."

"I'm experiencing minimal discomfort. At least in the vicinity of my wounds."

Obviously he considered her a pain in his posterior. Too bad. "These will ensure you won't have any pain at all, at least tonight. You'll sleep like a baby."

He nailed her with his fathomless black eyes. "And if I refuse?"

Of all the obstinate men. Good thing he was cute, otherwise she'd toss him out. "Then I'll do to you what I do with Lottie.

Grab your jaws and shove the pills in the back of your mouth, then rub your throat until you swallow.''

"You are determined to persist in this matter?"

"Yes, I am. So be a good boy and take them."

Releasing a frustrated sigh, he slid the pills from her palm, put them all in his mouth then swallowed the water. Fiona decided that even the bob of his Adam's apple was sexy. If only she had the courage to proposition him, as Peg had suggested, but she didn't. Not tonight. After all, he was wounded, and regardless of Peg's assertions that injuries wouldn't stop a man's ability to perform, Fiona was hard-pressed to believe it. Besides, tomorrow he would probably be gone. She'd never had a one-night stand. No need to start now.

Oh, well. Easy come, easy go.

"Open your mouth," she demanded. "I want to take a look and make sure you swallowed them."

"Do you not trust me?"

"Not exactly, so let me see."

With lightning speed, he clasped her wrists and pulled her forward between his parted legs. She planted her palms on his shoulders to keep from toppling into his lap, although that didn't seem like a totally abhorrent prospect. "How will you know for certain by using only your eyes?" he said in a deep, persuasive voice. "I could be hiding them."

"They would've dissolved by now." Her voice sounded like a rusty wheel.

"Perhaps, or perhaps not."

"Are you going to force me to pry your jaws open and put my hand in your mouth?"

His near-black eyes looked bedroom drowsy. "I would prefer you not put your hand in my mouth, but I would be open to other suggestions."

"I'm not quite sure I'm following you here, Scorpio."

He clasped the back of her head and pulled her closer, his lips only a fraction from hers. "You have other means to conduct a search."

Was he giving her an open invitation to engage in a little

tongue tango? That's what she thought he was doing, but she'd been wrong before. Better safe than really sorry. "You want me to do a little mouth-to-mouth expedition?"

"If you wish to know for certain, I see no other recourse."

Whew, boy. Peg had been right on. A near-death experience had done nothing to quell his manly urges. Or maybe it was the drugs. "Those pills are obviously doing their job if you want to kiss me."

"I have found your mouth quite fascinating from the moment we met. And since we are obviously stranded together for the evening, I propose we enjoy each other's company." His eyes closed, then slowly opened. "If you are willing."

Noting his words were somewhat slurred, she'd be darned if she'd do this with him when he was under the influence of painkillers. "We don't know each other."

"I know that you are a beautiful woman."

Beautiful? Now she knew he was high. "Come on, Scorpio. That's a stretch."

He slid his callused palms up and down her arms. "Are you calling me a liar?"

She was calling herself a fool for actually buying into this. "Believe me, I've heard many pickup lines from many men, enough to know that telling a woman she's beautiful is only a means to an end."

"I am not a man who uses false flattery to seduce a woman. True beauty cannot be hidden." His gaze tracked to her breasts then back to her eyes. "However, I will not force you into anything you do not wish to do."

His smile arrived, only halfway, but affected Fiona all the way. "Let's just say I do agree to do this. What's in for me?"

"You will have to find out."

She wanted to find out. Boy, did she want to. A little adventure. Just a little kiss.

Leaving common sense in the dust, she traced her tongue over the seam of his lips and without any coercion his mouth parted, giving her full advantage in this game of chance. Chances were meant to be taken, and she couldn't help believing that she was destined to kiss this man. And she did, with all the gusto of a woman who had done without this kind of intimacy for far too long.

But she didn't find any pills lurking on his tongue—a gentle, provocative tongue that stroked against hers until she thought she would collapse from a charisma overdose. She swayed forward and he brought her down on the sofa next to him in his strong arms.

Fiona didn't care that his evening whiskers abraded her chin. She didn't care that Lottie was in the next room, pitching a fit while her master was making out with a master kisser. A stranger no less. A stranger with one wicked tongue and one deliberate touch as he made light passes with his thumb over the side of her breast.

But soon he took his hand and his mouth away. Fiona opened her eyes to find him bowed forward, his elbows braced on his knees and his face in his palms.

"What did you give me?" he muttered.

She scooted to the edge of the cushion, her pulse pounding away like a jackhammer, this time from fear over his current condition. "Painkillers. They're supposed to be mild."

He fell back against the sofa. "Not mild enough. My head is spinning."

So was Fiona's, not only from his kiss but also from the fact that she'd drugged him into a stupor just when things were getting good. Worse, she might have really compromised his well-being.

She bolted from the sofa. "I need to call Peg."

He stretched out, and within seconds his eyes closed and his breathing grew steady.

Fiona grabbed the cordless phone from the end table and pounded out Peg's number. Before her neighbor could even say "Hello" she spewed the explanation about what she'd given Scorpio and how much, trying not to sound too panicked. Peg assured her that he wouldn't croak from taking two of that particular pill, but he would sleep soundly for several hours. In the meantime, she should watch him closely.

After Fiona hung up from Peg, she felt somewhat assured that she hadn't done Scorpio any real harm, and terribly disappointed that the evening had come to an abrupt halt. Probably just as well. She should have her head examined for actually kissing him, especially since she didn't even know him. But in some ways, that was the appeal. Doing something kind of risky, even if it was unwise. During her formative years, she'd had to be the logical one because of her mother's penchant for carefree living and questionable taste in men. Maybe it was more than time to live a little.

Lottie continued to whine and claw at the bedroom door. Worrying the noise might wake Scorpio, she coerced the dog from the bedroom with doggie bacon, intending to shut her in the kitchen with a bowl of water and a warning to use the newspaper. But before Fiona could stop her, Lottie bounded to the sofa and began bathing Scorpio's elbow with her black tongue, amazing since she wasn't all that fond of men. But this particular man wasn't like most men, and Lottie must have recognized that, too. Luckily, Scorpio didn't go for his gun, or even flinch for that matter. But that in itself concerned Fiona. What if he didn't wake up? What if she had inadvertently put him in a coma?

Fiona tugged Lottie into the kitchen, closed the door then went back into her bedroom to retrieve a decent blanket for the sleeping Scorpio now sprawled on his back, his limbs helter-skelter and the holey throw resting precariously low on his hips. At least he'd moved, Fiona thought. Before covering him, she laid her cheek against his chest, relieved to find he was still breathing. Just the feel of his warm flesh against her face made her want to stay that way indefinitely, listening to the steady beat of his heart. Instead, she pulled up a chair to watch him, pondering how anyone so incredibly masculine could look so innocent in sleep. So undeniably gorgeous with those angelic eyelashes and heavenly lips. After a few minutes, he shifted slightly, groaned, then rolled away to face the back of the sofa, ending her pleasant observations.

She kept vigil for over two hours, observing the rise and

fall of his back then his chest, depending on what position he assumed, and he'd assumed plenty. As best she could tell, he seemed restless but okay. At times he tossed and turned, other times he murmured words she couldn't understand as if something was disturbing his sleep. Probably bad dreams of nasty villains and the chase.

Satisfied that she hadn't permanently disabled him, Fiona trudged into the bathroom, took a quick shower and climbed into bed, leaving the door ajar in case he needed her during what little was left of the night. And here she was, alone, when a striking representative of the male populace with a made-for-fun body and a mouth that matched, was only a few yards away, and naked to boot. A man she had put into a deep sleep.

The story of her sad, sad life. But at least tomorrow morning she could take one last look at him before she left for class and he left to pursue the dregs of society. If he was in any shape to leave. Considering the extent of his ankle injury, she would be darned surprised if he could walk, much less chase the evil Dr. B. Not without help. Not without someone willing to take a risk to help him. Someone who wanted adventure.

Fiona popped up, held her arms above her head and mouthed a silent, ''Yes!''

She had his car keys and she had his clothes. He couldn't go anywhere unless she gave them back, and she wouldn't unless he agreed to let her assist him. She would offer to show him the dark side of the city, the perfect hiding places, and any other sights he might want to see that didn't include standard tourism.

Fiona planned to take this quest to the max, and she expected to get a wild ride in return with the stranger named Scorpio, in bed and out.

Three

Fiona's eyes snapped open when she felt the give of the mattress behind her. She glanced at the bedside alarm clock, noting it was 6:00 a.m. Either Lottie had nosed her way through the pocket door, ready for her morning walk, or the stranger on the couch had somehow made his way to her bed. Normally even the wisp of the wind or the creak of the upstairs floorboard under her noisy neighbor's weight sent her into wakefulness. Surely if Scorpio had climbed beneath her sheets, she would've noticed.

But when the large, very masculine arm fell over Fiona's hip, she knew for a fact it wasn't her precocious puppy occupying the space beside her. Absolute confirmation came when his body molded to her backside, bringing her in close contact with the patently male missile.

Houston, we have liftoff.

Fiona had several choices. She could bolt from the bed and pretend to be incensed over his boldness. She could slide from the bed and offer him breakfast. Or she could stay put and see what happened next—and that certainly seemed like the most exciting option.

The feel of his lips, hot and damp at her nape, led Fiona to the realization that he wasn't seeking coffee and a croissant. His hand working her cotton nightshirt up her thighs indicated that he might be looking for something a bit more decadent. When his palm slid beneath the shirt and up her torso, she had no problem letting him play traveling salesman over her body since she was more than ready to buy whatever he was offering.

His large hand closed over her bare breast and worked her nipple with gentle fingertips, with surprising tenderness for a man who'd seemed the consummate tough guy. No doubt about it, he'd done this before, probably many times with many different women, one very solid reason why she should *not* be allowing this to continue. Yet when he skimmed his palm down from her breast to her belly, ran his tongue around the rim of her ear, she tossed caution to the wind and held her breath in anticipation.

"Tamra."

Tamra? Who in the heck was Tamra?

Fiona pushed out of the bed and faced him, recognizing he hadn't been awake at all, evident by his slack features and the way his dark arm lay motionless against the white sheet, his eyes tightly closed. He hadn't even realized she'd left. Hadn't even realized he'd been touching her. In his subconscious, she had been someone else. Someone who obviously haunted his dreams. Tamra, not Fiona.

Maybe he'd lied to her about having no ties. Maybe this Tamra was his wife or girlfriend. Heaven knew she'd seen enough subterfuge in the bar to fill a book dedicated to devious deception. And if he had lied to her, then what else was he lying about? Was he really one of the good guys? She certainly intended to find out, hopefully before he woke up completely.

Fiona tiptoed into the bathroom and dressed in a pair of faded black knit shorts, a light blue ''You Can't Touch

These" T-shirt and red canvas mules. If the clothing cops arrived in the parking lot, she'd warrant a citation. Better them than the oh-so-demented Dr. B.

With stealth movements, Fiona backed into the living room, satisfied to find that Mr. Scorpio was still in la-la land. She dug into her purse, retrieved the keys and slipped out the front door feeling a bite of remorse over leaving poor Lottie whining in the kitchen and a little guilty over what she was about to do. But this was for self-protection. She had a unfamiliar person—granted a really good-looking one—in her bed and she was more than justified in checking out his belongings. Especially since she'd already checked out his butt.

After making her way to the parking space she'd pulled into last night, Fiona tripped the latch on the white four-door sedan with the remote and pulled the nylon tote from the trunk. Black tote, of course. She thought it the better part of valor to poke around in the parking lot in case he should wake up and catch her. That might make him angry, and she certainly didn't want to have him angry with her.

She pushed aside more black clothing, socks, pants, shirts but no drawers. Obviously the guy preferred to go commando, maybe because he was always on the run. Less to have to dress in. Then she came to a wallet that was amazingly brown and rifled through the contents, discovering that he carried a lot of cash, mostly hundreds. Drug money? Oh, Lord, she hoped not.

When the bag began to ring, Fiona jumped and dropped the wallet, scattering the bills throughout the trunk. The shrill continued and she unzipped one side pocket, pulled out the biggest handkerchief she'd ever seen and some sort of gold band, finally withdrawing a cell phone. Should she answer it? Oh, why not. After all, she didn't need to leave any stone, or phone, unturned.

Fiona answered with a simple "Hello," and was immediately met with silence. She repeated the greeting again and this time a deep voice said, "I must have the wrong number."

"Probably not if you're looking for Scorpio."

After a long pause he asked, "Who is this?"

"You go first."

"I'm a colleague of Darin's."

Darin? Aha! The first lie uncovered. "Are you a cop, too?"

"In a manner of speaking. What is your relationship with him?"

"I'm a friend." A big lie considering she was doing something that wouldn't be considered too friendly, namely going through his things. She tucked the phone between her cheek and shoulder then began gathering the money, stuffing it back into the wallet. "Darin is asleep right now. Could I take a message?"

"You need to wake him."

Fiona grimaced over the man's demanding tone. Must be a law-enforcement thing. "That might be a problem. He's pretty out of it."

His impatient sigh followed another bout of silence. "Could you possibly try, Ms.…?"

"Powers. And yes, I can try, but he's really wiped out after last night."

"What transpired last night?"

She considered giving him details, but how did she know she could trust this guy, either? "Maybe I should let Darin tell you."

"Ms. Powers, it's important I speak with him immediately."

"Why don't you let me take your name and number and have him call you when he gets up?"

More silence, followed by, "Tell him Kent called. He knows the number."

With that, the line went dead, leaving Fiona with more questions and no answers. She replaced the wallet, hanky and phone then returned his clothes to some semblance of order. Slipping the bag's strap over her shoulder, she shut the trunk and headed back to the apartment to prepare some coffee and toast since she had no croissants. And as soon as Sleeping Babe woke up, she would offer him food and grill him like a drill sergeant. If his explanations passed muster, she would give him the bag...after he agreed to let her help him.

On that thought, she dropped the car keys into the pocket of her shorts. If he wanted them, he'd have to go get them.

Darin woke in slow increments, unable to orientate himself to time or place. Remnants of a dream assailed him, vague images of making love, and one part of his body still suffered the effects.

He rose on bent elbows and looked around to find a woman sitting in a chair in the corner of the small bedroom. The woman named Fiona who had taken him into her home and tended his wounds. The one who had drugged him into a near coma.

She sent him a vibrant smile. "Did you sleep well, *Darin*?"

Apparently he had told her more than he'd realized, perhaps while in his confused state. "How do you know my true name?"

"Well, I was getting your bag out of the trunk of the car and your cell phone rang, so I decided to answer it. Your friend named Kent wants you to call him."

Darin dropped back onto the pillow and stared at the ceiling, the wound at his ankle a dull throb to match the pain in his head. "What did he say?"

"Not much. He asked me a few questions. I interrogated him. Overall, it wasn't a banner conversation. He did want to know what happened last night."

His gaze snapped to hers. "What did you tell him?"

"I told him he needed to ask you. He sounded kind of mad."

Darin suspected Alex had learned that he had not connected with the FBI agent and most likely was not too pleased. "I will speak with him later about last night."

"Do you even remember what happened last night?"

He remembered every detail of his pursuit of Birkenfeld and his failure. He also remembered that the drugs she'd given him had provided courage to act on his desire for her. And he definitely remembered how she had tasted, her enthusiastic response and his own body's reaction before he had slipped into unconsciousness. But to express anything beyond his gratitude for her assistance would be unwise. He must leave immediately to continue his search for Birkenfeld. He had no time for distraction.

· Therefore, he would only tell her a partial truth. "I remember up to the point that I took the pills. After that, I remember nothing."

Disappointment showed in her expression. "You don't remember getting up and crawling into bed with me?"

He remembered searching for something in his dreams, or someone. "No. I am surprised I could walk, much less see in the dark."

"Maybe your injuries aren't all that bad. At least you didn't seem to be in any real pain before you passed out."

In reality, he'd had an ache that had nothing to do with his wounds. He still experienced a certain amount of discomfort when he couldn't seem to stop his gaze from tracking from her full lips to her full breasts that he greatly wanted to touch, despite the warning stamped across the front of the shirt. "I assure you, I slept very well. I am grateful for your aid although I do not appreciate the power of the drugs. If Birkenfeld had come here, I would not have been in any shape to deal with him."

"But I was fine, and I had access to your gun."

"Would you know how to use it?"

"I would've figured it out, Scorpio. Or should I just call you Darin?"

"You may call me whatever you wish." He called himself a fool since he had the strongest urge to grab her up and take her into the bed, strip away her clothes and bury himself inside her. Despite the fact that he no longer suffered from the narcotics, he was no less attracted to her. And unless he left her soon, he was in serious danger of acting on the fantasy of making love to her, all day, when he had more pressing matters to attend to aside from the one below the sheet.

She moved forward to the edge of the chair. "I have a question for you."

More questions he wasn't certain he could answer. "Yes?"

"Who's Tamra?"

The name sent a pain slicing through Darin's heart more severe than Birkenfeld's blade. "Where did you hear that name?" His tone was harsher than he'd intended.

"You called me Tamra this morning."

Darin feared he had done more than that. "Did I touch you?"

She looked away. "A little."

He sighed. "Then that would explain my dream."

Her gaze came back to his. "Was it dirty?"

"In a manner of speaking."

A slight smile rounded the corners of her mouth then quickly faded. "You still haven't told me who Tamra is."

"Someone I once knew." Someone he'd once loved and in many ways still did.

"But she's not your wife?"

"No." She would have been, had things been different, but he would not reveal that to Fiona. He would not let himself open those wounds.

"She must have been special if you still talk about her in your sleep. If you still dream about her."

And Darin found that odd. To his best recollection, he had not dreamed about Tamra, although he had on many occasions over the past few years. "She was part of my past. A past that no longer exists."

"Okay." She rose from the chair. "Would you like some coffee and toast?"

Darin sat up and his head felt as if it had been stuffed with cotton. His body was sore from the effort, which did not bode well for the search. Nor did the fact that he couldn't stop imagining Fiona beneath him. "Coffee would be good before I leave."

Fiona studied him with concern. "You look really awful. I'm wondering if you lost more blood than we thought. Maybe you should plan to stick around here today."

"I must find Birkenfeld."

She braced both hands on her hips and sent him a frustrated look. "You really think he's going to just appear in the day-time?"

He did not appreciate her logic, yet he did appreciate the view of her well-defined legs, bare because of the shorts she now wore. "I can spend the day planning."

"You can plan here. I have a class in a few hours so I won't bother you. I'll make sure Lottie's locked up so she won't bother you, either."

"I would not want to impose further on your hospitality." Darin worked his way to the edge of the mattress, keeping the sheet securely covering his body. "Bring me my bag, and I will dress and be out of your way."

"No."

She was determined to be difficult, that much Darin knew. And his patience was waning. "What do you mean 'no'?"

"I mean, no, I will not get your bag. You are in no shape to be running all over Vegas by yourself."

"I have always worked alone."

"Sure, but I doubt you had a bum ankle." She pulled at the hem of her T-shirt, drawing the fabric tight over her un-bound breasts. "Besides, you don't really know where to look."

Darin could only stare at her nipples, pebbled beneath her shirt. And that simple sight sent heat coursing through him. "I have done some research."

She released a mirthless laugh. "Did you pull up a few Web sites on the Internet? What did you search under? Seedy Vegas bars?"

"No." But he did have a few names of people he could contact if necessary. Those who would not be deemed up-standing citizens. "I'll find my way around, I assure you."

"Good luck. But I'm still not going to get your bag."

Fueled by frustration over her stubbornness, Darin rose from the bed, discarding the sheet in hopes of shocking her into returning his clothes. Yet she remained planted in the same spot, arms folded beneath her breasts as if viewing a nude man was a common event. Perhaps it was, and for some reason that fed Darin's anger more, as if he had some claim on her.

He took a stalking step forward. "Are you going to give me my clothing, or shall I walk to the car naked on my injured ankle?"

When her gaze followed a path from his chest down his abdomen and below his navel, he hardened more over her blatant perusal.

"I do believe you have one part that's definitely in fine working order," she said.

"Would you like to find out how well it is working?"

She didn't back away, but she did consult her watch. "Sorry. Got to get ready for school now. Maybe later?"

"I'll be gone later."

Her smile arrived full force as she fished through her pocket and withdrew his keys, dangling them from one finger. "You'll be here unless you call a cab or set out on foot. A bad foot, I might add. And although Vegas cab drivers are used to strange phenomena, I really don't think they're going to pick up a naked man. Unless, of course, you're lucky enough to find a woman cab driver. But then you would have to pay her without the benefit of money because I have your wallet and your clothes."

It would be easy for him to grab the keys from her. Easy to persuade her to relinquish them in ways that did not include force. For some reason he made no move to take the keys or her…yet. "You are determined to hold me hostage?"

"For a little while. I also need to borrow your car since mine won't be ready until tomorrow morning. I think that's the least you can do considering what I did for you last night."

Darin was caught between desire and fury. He wanted to

shake some sense into her. He wanted to carry her to the bed and take off her clothing so they were both naked. "I find your behavior unwarranted. I'm not certain why you are even concerned over my well-being."

She slipped the keys back into her pocket. "You know something, Scorpio, I'm not sure, either, other than you saved my life. You're pretty darned demanding. Sexy but demanding."

Darin took another step toward her and a sharp pain shot up from his ankle to the back of his leg, but this time it did nothing to quell his lust. "*I* am demanding?"

"Okay, maybe I can relate. And that's why I'm going to help you find this Birkenfeld guy."

The woman had taken total leave of her senses. "I will not allow it."

"Oh, yeah, you will. If you ever want to see your clothes, money and car again." She gestured toward the living area. "You'll find a pot of coffee in the kitchen. Have some. Maybe then you'll be in a better mood." With one more direct look at his erection that had yet to calm, she pivoted on her heels and headed into the bathroom.

Darin doubted that coffee would alleviate his foul mood. He had been bested by a woman—a woman who was at least a foot shorter and one hundred pounds lighter. A woman whose tenacity both angered and excited him. Regardless, he would not accept her assistance in finding Birkenfeld. He refused to put another woman in the path of danger—even a woman who could probably wrestle a Bengal tiger with her bare hands...and bring Darin to his knees with only a kiss.

She should have known he wouldn't remember the kiss.

That afternoon Fiona mulled it over and over on her drive back to the apartment following her classes, convinced Scorpio's amorous behavior the night before had been a result of the pills. How nice to know that she'd had to rely on mood-altering drugs in order to seduce a man. Peg would be very disappointed.

However, Fiona had to admit that Scorpio seemed quite
with it this morning, not under the influence at all when he'd
shown her his stuff. And some stuff it was. It had taken all
her restraint not to gasp and keel over when he crawled from
the bed and dropped the sheet. At least she hadn't dropped to
her knees. But she had felt as if she'd ingested a tanker full
of Mexican tequila. Had it not been for the death grip she'd
maintained on her will, or the fact that he'd been wounded,
she might have tackled him and forgotten all about her class.
But she was too close to finishing school to let a man side-
track her. That had been her mother's favorite trick.

As she pulled in front of her apartment, Fiona wondered if
he was still around. Scorpio struck her as being a resourceful
guy, and she wouldn't be a bit surprised if he'd fashioned a
bath towel into some sort of combat gear, then set out on his
own in the streets of Vegas with his feet crammed into her
sneakers that would definitely be too small. He certainly
wouldn't fit into her clothes since he was so big. Every part
of him.

But she had noticed he hadn't been walking all that well,
although he'd tried to hide his distress—the only thing he'd
kept hidden from her. She shivered again just thinking about
the picture he'd presented standing by her bed covered only
by dark skin, random patches of masculine hair while sporting
a challenging look and proof positive of his arousal. And if
she kept thinking about that, she would never be able to look
him in the face again.

Fiona could only hope that he had decided to stick around
after recognizing the extent of his injuries and the logic of her
offer. Funny, he hadn't put up that much of a fight when she'd
taunted him with the keys. No doubt he could have taken her
down on the floor and had them in his possession in a matter
of moments, despite his injuries. That might have been really,
really fun. She probably wouldn't have put up much of a fight,
either, especially if he'd decided to possess her.

What a fantasy, one that she needed to forget. Scorpio was
determined to go catch a bad guy, not catch a quick roll with

her. Unless he changed his mind later. Maybe she might try
to change it for him.

Good grief. In less than twenty-four hours, she'd gone from
single celibate to single-minded femme fatale. Her mother
would be so proud.

Fiona slid out of the car and pushed into the apartment to
find her guest stretched out on the sofa, wearing a mint-
colored terry towel around his waist and a detached expression. Even after she closed the door, he kept his eyes centered
on the television, where some kind of soap opera involving a
lot of heaving breasts and heavy breathing between a couple
in a hot tub played out on the screen. What a novel idea, but
she didn't have a hot tub. In fact, she only had a shower.

She also had an enamored canine who had managed to take
up residence at the end of the sofa, chin resting on Scorpio's
bare shin. Normally the dog would have been shaking all over
from excitement when Fiona came in. Instead, Lottie had
barely looked up. No surprise. Scorpio would have that effect
on females of any species.

Fiona tossed the keys on the table then on afterthought, put
them back in her jeans pocket. "How was your day, honey?
Did you enjoy the lunch I made for you?"

Domestic goddess she was not, but it was a pretty darned
good imitation.

Scorpio did not appreciate her attempt at playing happy
housewife, very apparent by his scowl. "I did not eat any
lunch since your hound beat me to it. I greatly underestimated
her ability to climb."

"Let me guess. You put it on the table then turned your
back?"

"Yes."

Uh-oh. "I forgot to warn you she'll go to great lengths to
steal food."

Lottie raised her head and cocked it to one side, displaying
her well-practiced Who Me? look.

"You must be starving, then," Fiona said, hoping to make

amends for her dog's lack of manners. "We'll have an early dinner. I'll get it started."

He slicked a hand over his scalp and leveled his dark gaze on her. "That will not be necessary. If you give me my clothes, I will be on my way."

Fiona gritted her teeth to keep from shouting. "You need something to eat, otherwise you're going to drop in your tracks."

"In the past, I have survived without food for days at time."

"And I'd bet you hadn't lost a lot of blood, either."

He fairly unfolded from the sofa and perched on the edge of the cushions. "I am feeling better."

"Prove it."

He grinned, taking Fiona by surprise. "How would you wish me to do that?"

Heat shot like a rocket from low in her belly, then landed on her face. "I was going to suggest you walk across the room, unless you have something else in mind."

"I was wondering the same about you."

Now was her chance. She could tell him exactly what was on her mind and let the chips—and the towel—fall where they may, followed by her clothes. But not yet. Not until he agreed to let her help him. She would withhold any kind of sexual suggestion and use that as an additional trump card. Like that would really entice him to hang around. She could try.

"I've come up with a plan, Scorpio." Strolling to the sofa, she stood immediately before him and smiled. "Do you mind if I just keep calling you Scorpio?"

"No, I do not mind."

"Good." My gosh, his face was gorgeous, even this close. "Why don't you let me show you a few places tonight?"

He kept his hands clasped tightly in his lap. "Places?"

"Bars. Places only someone without good sense or a death wish would visit."

"What about your job?"

"I'm off on Tuesdays and Wednesdays."

"I've told you I do not want to put you in danger."

"You won't be putting me in any danger. If we do happen to find the bad guy, then I'll stand back and let you do your thing. Besides, people trust me. They won't tell you anything if they think you're law enforcement."

"And if I do not agree to this plan? What will you do then?"

She grinned. "I think you should consider what I *will* do if you let me help."

He hinted at another smile. "Prepare dinner?"

"Sure. And I'll provide some dessert after we get back."

His eyes darkened to extremes as he gripped her waist in his very strong, very big hands. "Your offer is tempting, but I am still concerned about your safety."

"You shouldn't be concerned. I can hold my own in most situations." She sent a pointed look at the obvious bulge beneath the towel.

His expression turned serious. "After this investigation is over, I do not plan to stay."

The old I'm-footloose-and-fancy-free speech. Fiona had heard other women discuss it, but this was a first for her. "I realize that."

"And I will only allow you limited participation."

"I prefer to participate to the fullest extent," she said, hoping she sounded sultry, not silly. "Some things are best done together. Much more fun that way."

"I was referring to the search for Birkenfeld."

She faked an innocent look. Lottie would be so proud. "Of course. You're the expert there. I'll do whatever you ask me to do."

He raised a dark brow. "Anything?"

Fiona's heart rate picked up speed. "As long as it's legal in most states."

He cupped her bottom and pulled her between his parted knees. "You are comfortable with taking risks?"

"Nothing ventured, nothing gained."

"Then perhaps we should have a meal and get started when it's dark outside."

"Don't you know it's never really dark in Vegas?" Oh, but his eyes were dark. Dark and deadly to a woman who had naughty things on her mind. Secretive eyes. Seductive.

She stepped away before she lost her will to stand firm since he had yet to agree to her proposal. "Dinner will only take a few minutes. I hope you like pasta."

He caught her wrist and pulled forward again. She had to grab his shoulders to keep from falling, although she was already falling into a sensual abyss that she didn't want to escape. "I would like to seal our agreement with another kiss," he said, his voice deep and enticing.

Another kiss? "You do remember last night."

"I was not that intoxicated. At least not from the effects of the drugs."

With one large palm, he brought her head down and kissed her with the same ardor he'd displayed the night before. Fiona wanted to lock the door, lock out the world, lock Lottie in the kitchen and stay this way indefinitely, experiencing the heat of his mouth and the skill of his tongue, the softness of his lips. She didn't want to chase a bad guy; she wanted to be bad with this guy.

Scorpio had other ideas. He let her go and this time he wasn't smiling. "Now bring me my clothes."

Fiona stepped back again. "Oh, so you kissed me in exchange for your clothes?"

"I kissed you because you looked as if you wanted to be kissed."

She rolled her eyes. "I'll give them to you after dinner. I want to make sure you stay around for a while."

"I am a man of my word, Fiona. I will adhere to our agreement, unless I suspect that you are in danger."

She was already in danger. In danger of totally falling for this seriously sexy man. And that was a danger she couldn't afford because she knew he wouldn't stay.

Four

"**O**kay, Scorpio. This is the next stop on the Investigation Express."

After Fiona pulled into the crowded parking lot and took a space several rows from the entrance, Darin studied the bright pink-and-green neon billboard that heralded live dancing girls and affordable drinks, as well as the depiction of a caricature cat-woman dressed in western attire. The two previous bars had been less than desirable establishments, but Darin would deem the Frisky Kitty Nightclub as the worst of the worst.

"You believe Birkenfeld would come to a place where women remove their clothing for pay?" he asked.

Fiona put the car in park. "Sure, unless he doesn't like women."

"He uses women. He kidnapped one and held her for ransom. Fortunately, she was rescued before he could harm her."

Fiona hesitated, as if mulling over the information. "Let me get this straight. He's a murderer, a baby thief, a fugitive *and* he kidnaps women?"

"That is correct."

"I would classify him as too abominable to live."

Darin was definitely in agreement. But it would not be up to him to mete out the punishment of death—unless circumstances called for it. "I will see him brought to justice. If not tonight, then soon."

"Well, this is a good place for him to blend in. Mostly locals. No blackjack tables, but it does have a good selection of one-armed bandits."

He couldn't resist teasing her. "Criminals with only one arm?"

"Slot machines, Scorpio. And don't think I don't know you've seen one before."

When Fiona tripped the lock and opened her door, Darin told her, "Perhaps you should remain here."

She shifted to face him. "Look, Darin dear, I'm not thrilled about going in there because I'm probably going to be the only woman wearing any clothes. But I know the bartender and he'll talk to me. So you're just going to have to accept the fact that I'm not going to sit all night in a parking lot waiting for you."

Once more, her resolve frustrated him. Yet he realized she had made a valid point. "Stay close to me," he said as he opened his door and slid out. When his foot hit the graveled surface, his ankle almost buckled. He was having difficulty maintaining his balance and he suspected Fiona had noticed.

She rounded the hood, came to his side and pulled his arm over her shoulder, confirming his suspicions. "Lean on me and act like you like it."

He did like it, very much so. "This is not necessary."

"Yes, it is. First, we'll appear to be a couple. Second, you won't have to worry about falling on your cute butt."

He stared down at her. "Cute?"

"I think it's an appropriate adjective, but I can come up with a few more if you'd like. Later."

Darin had been engaging in a battle to control his desire since the moment he'd met her. That battle had not subsided during dinner, but he had controlled his urges in the car even though Fiona had dressed in a black leather skirt that revealed her shapely legs and a tight sleeveless white blouse that enhanced her breasts. Yet if she kept making promises about what would transpire later, he would be forced to close his jacket in order to hide his sinful musings.

"I hate wearing skirts and heels," Fiona muttered as they crossed the lot.

Darin, on the other hand, greatly appreciated her attire. "They why did you choose to wear them?"

"I'm trying to look like a woman enjoying a night on the town. I'm afraid I look like a fish out of water, or someone who's trying to earn a few bucks turning tricks." She glanced at him. "But you don't look like a guy who'd have to pay for it."

She looked like a wild fantasy with her red hair curling about her face. "I suppose I should be flattered."

"You definitely should."

Fiona pulled open the heavy door and stepped inside first, then once more wrapped her arm around his waist. He kept his arm draped over her shoulder, trying to ignore the pain in his thigh and ankle resulting from the distance they'd had to travel to reach the entry. How would he give chase if he did find Birkenfeld? He only had to get close enough to take a shot. His hand automatically brushed across the holster concealed by his jacket, finding some comfort in knowing he had the means to protect himself, and Fiona, should they encounter the doctor.

A fog of smoke hung over the bar, and loud music boomed from speakers set out in the room. A woman wearing only a silver G-string whirled around a pole rising from the middle of a stage while several men whistled and called out to her, her expression almost impassive.

Darin had seen it before, a face that showed the signs of a difficult life and a blank demeanor to mask all emotions, as if she had tuned everyone and everything out in order to get through the routine. Darin could relate. Many times he'd gone through the motions of living to block out the pain. Admittedly he was not immune to her seductive moves, yet his desire was not for this woman but the one at his side now working her way through hordes of men taking in the spectacle. Several leered at Fiona, angering Darin. Under most circumstances, he would risk starting a brawl to defend her honor. But he could not risk drawing attention to them if Birkenfeld happened to be on the premises, something he greatly doubted.

Fiona guided him to the bar where they took seats on the stools, side by side. She smiled as if she had entered the Taj Mahal, not a tavern. Where Darin had become jaded with life, Fiona reveled in it. Her passion for living showed in every move she made, in every word, even those that didn't please him. She was eight years his junior, but after the cruelty he'd seen, Darin felt as if they were separated by decades. Although his initial attraction to her involved pure primal lust, her optimism drew him now, on a deeper level. If only he could be so sanguine.

"Lookin' good tonight, Fiona," a man with myriad tattoos covering much of his massive arms called out from behind the bar. He moved in front of Fiona to kiss her cheek, and she responded with a deeper smile and a friendly, "You're looking fine tonight, too, Mort."

When the man continued to assess Fiona as if he owned her, Darin took Fiona's hand into his, a show of possession intended to convince the bartender they were a couple. Yet the surge of jealousy spiraling through Darin seemed surprisingly real. He had no cause to concern himself over Fiona's friends or her activities. She was only with him now because she had insisted and he had agreed. Still, he did not like the way this Mort kept eyeing Fiona with obvious lust, as if he did have designs on her and no respect for the fact she was with another.

Fiona flipped a hand in Darin's direction. "Mort, this is my friend…" She looked at him as if uncertain what to call him.

Darin reluctantly offered his hand but no smile. "Frank."

The man nodded. "Nice to meet you, Frank. What brings you two here tonight?"

Fiona leaned forward and said, "Frank is looking for a guy who owes him money. He's about six-two, beady brown eyes, shaved head. Goes by the name Birkenfeld."

"Or possibly Belden," Darin added, the name of the doctor Birkenfeld had murdered to assume his identity.

"Don't know him personally," Mort said. "But then that describes several guys around here. Anything else specific you can give me?"

Darin pulled the mug shot from his pocket. "This was taken before he shaved his head."

Mort wiped his hands on a towel, took the picture and studied it. "Matter of fact, I think I might have seen him in here."

Fiona's expression brightened. "When?"

"Just a few minutes ago."

Darin was cautiously optimistic. "Where?"

The bartender nodded toward the far side of the room. "Corner table. But I don't want no trouble, so take it outside."

Fiona swiveled on the stool to face Darin. "Do you want me to go over there and check it out?"

Darin leaned over and lowered his voice. "No. He might recognize you."

Fiona toyed with a silver chain circling her delicate throat. "The alley was dark that night."

"Not dark enough. He would remember you."

A sigh of annoyance slipped out of her pursed lips. "Then what do you propose we do?"

"Wait. He will have to pass by here in order to exit."

"That could take all night."

"And that is what much of this business is about. Waiting. You may return to the apartment. I will call you if I need you."

"No way." She stared at the woman who now worked the

perimeter of the stage while men stuffed bills in her G-string. "Look at those guys. They're practically drooling like Lottie with a bone."

Darin could only look at Fiona, her pleasing profile, up-turned nose and delicate neck that he wanted to kiss, badly.

One disheveled, staggering man walking by the bar paused to look Fiona over, then said, "I'll tip you real good if you'll dance for me, baby."

Darin's ears began to ring. "She is not—"

"Going to dance," Fiona interrupted. "But I will give you a tip. Pointed, high heels in the area of the family jewels can bring a man down in about five seconds."

The lecher sneered. "Bitch."

Darin tried to come off the stool when the miscreant started away, but Fiona stopped him with an arm across his chest. "Let it go. He's not worth your bother. Remember why we're here."

Darin despised that he had forgotten, several times now, this mission and his goals. Yet he would have gladly splattered the bastard's nose all over his face, then resumed his duty.

Fiona took Darin's hand and rested it on her thigh exposed by the skirt's upward climb as she crossed one leg over the other. "I just had a thought."

So had Darin and it involved finding out what she was wearing beneath that skirt. "A thought?"

"More like a plan. We should wait in the car so he doesn't see us and try to run out the back way. We could pull up closer to the building in the handicapped spot."

"That would require a permit."

"Yeah, but if anyone questions it, all we have to do is have you walk a few steps."

Darin did not wish to be reminded of his current hindrance although the aching wounds would not let him forget. Nor could he discard the other ache low in his groin as the music began again and another woman took to the stage, engaging in a suggestive dance directed at the patrons lining the stage.

"You two want anything to drink?" the bartender asked.

"No," Fiona said, and slipped the strap of her purse over her shoulder. "We're going to go outside and wait in the car."

Mort grinned. "The car, huh? Is this a private party or can anyone join?"

Darin fought the urge to wipe the smirk off Mort's face with his fist. He sent the bartender an acrid look, then pulled Fiona off the stool and held her securely against his side. "It is private."

The man had the nerve to wink at Fiona. "I always knew a real party girl was hiding beneath that great body of yours, Fee."

With one arm still wrapped around Fiona, Darin leaned over the bar and said, "Her body should not concern you."

The man held his hands up, palms forward in surrender. "Chill, dude. I'm just yanking Fiona's chain a little."

"It's okay, *Frankie,*" Fiona said. "Mort's one of the good guys, too."

Darin ignored her sarcasm then nudged her forward and out the door. Once on the walkway, Fiona wrenched away and faced him with wrath.

"Did you really have to act like such a jerk? Mort was just joking."

Darin started across the parking lot, limping as quickly as his ankle would allow, Fiona following closely behind him. "He was not joking, I assure you. It's very difficult to ignore your body considering your clothing."

Fiona grabbed his arm and turned him around. "What's wrong with my clothes?"

"Nothing, and that is the problem." Darin continued on and when they reached the car, Fiona slipped inside before he'd barely had a chance to open his door. For a moment he feared she might take off before he had the opportunity to sit.

They drove to the handicapped parking space near the front door without speaking. After Fiona turned off the ignition, the silence continued for a few moments before she said, "You sounded almost jealous in there."

Unfortunately, she was correct. "I only intended to protect you from unwanted overtures."

Fiona released a sharp laugh. "Unwanted overtures? Protect me? I don't need your protection from my friends! Do you hear me?"

"Yes, quite clearly, and I imagine so did the rest of the patrons in the bar."

She looked somewhat contrite. "I wasn't talking that loudly."

Darin couldn't suppress his smile. "It was only a mild shout."

She slapped at his arm. "You are so…so…"

"Observant?"

"Frustrating."

Darin was experiencing his own frustration. Sexual frustration. Fiona had not adjusted her skirt, sending him on an imaginary journey that included running his palms up her bare thighs and much higher.

"It's very warm in here," he said, his voice hinting at that frustration.

"I'll roll down the windows."

"Only partway," he cautioned.

She glared at him when his eyes followed the path he greatly wanted to take with his hands and mouth. "Anything else I can do for you?" she asked.

He could think of several things but most would be difficult to manage in the close confines of a sedan, although it could be managed if he had better mobility. "Help me keep watch for Birkenfeld."

Fiona remained silent for a brief time before saying, "So this is what a stakeout is all about? Just sitting here, watching a door?"

"Yes."

"Not very exciting."

"But necessary."

She drummed her fingertips on the steering wheel. "Can I turn on the radio?"

"No."

"Why not? Is music too distracting?"

She was too distracting. "I would know his voice if I heard it. I cannot hear it if music is blaring from the radio."

"I'll keep it low. Besides, you'll probably see him before—"

He halted her words by placing his hand over her mouth. "Someone's coming out the door. Keep your voice down."

She yanked his hand away. "Why? They'll just think we're having an argument. A common lovers' quarrel, which looks a little less obvious than us just sitting here, staring like we're in a stupor."

"We are not lovers." Yet.

The words hung heavy in the car as they watched a man and woman exit the building, arms about each other, their laughter filtering into the partially opened windows. Once the couple passed by the hood of the car, Fiona pushed the seat backward, toed out of her high heels then tossed them aside. She curled one leg beneath her and leaned back against the door, raising her hem higher on her thighs, endangering Darin's concentration.

"Tell me something, Scorpio. Does that turn you on, seeing women dancing around wearing next to nothing?"

"I paid little attention to them."

She released an abrupt laugh. "Yeah, right. Since when does a man not notice a naked woman gyrating in the middle of an elevated stage?"

"I had more important things on my mind."

"Such as?"

Removing Fiona's clothing. "Apprehending Birkenfeld."

She sent him a doubtful look. "Even a naked woman can't distract you?"

"That would depend on the woman."

She gestured toward the building. "What about that second dancer? You have to admit, she was very attractive. Which really puzzles me. Why would a woman who looks like that choose to make a living stripping?''

"Perhaps she believes she has no other skills to make a living.''

"I've never had much money and I've survived without resorting to taking off my clothes for money.''

"Maybe she wishes to do it.''

"Are you saying she enjoys it?''

"That would not be unheard of.''

Fiona again fondled the chain above her breasts, drawing Darin's attention and fueling his arousal. "I guess that could be a rush, stripping for a man. But only one man, not fifty.''

Darin allowed his gaze to slowly roam over her. "I'm certain many men would greatly appreciate you removing your clothing for them.''

Her expression was a combination of sultry seductress with a hint of self-consciousness. "How about you?''

"Most definitely.'' If they were anywhere else, doing anything else, he would suggest she remove her clothing for him now.

Taking Darin by surprise, Fiona raised her right leg and propped a heel on the console between them. "I have a cramp in my foot,'' she said as she kneaded her instep. "Must be those darned high heels.''

When he saw the flash of black silk between her legs, Darin greatly wanted to offer her assistance. Greatly wanted to run his palm from the back of her knee down her thigh. But he wouldn't stop there. He would keep going until she begged him for mercy. And he would gladly give it to her.

Fiona dropped her foot before Darin could act on the impulse and stared out the windshield. "Someone's coming.''

Darin forced his gaze to the entry to find Mort filling the doorway with another man standing before him—a man with a shaved head, all the details Darin could discern since the stranger had his back to the car. Every nerve in Darin's body, every well-honed instinct went on maximum alert when the bartender gestured toward the parking lot. Darin sank down into the seat, shoved the cap lower on his brow, then reached over and grabbed Fiona by the nape, pulling her head down into his lap. "Do not move," he told her as he slid his hand beneath the jacket and withdrew the gun.

The stranger turned toward the car. He resembled Birkenfeld, but Darin would never forget the doctor's demonic eyes, hard, void of emotion. This man's eyes were smaller, full of confusion but not absolute evil.

"It is not him," he told Fiona whose cheek now rested on his thigh.

"Wonderful. Can I get up now?"

Darin stared down on her as the heat of her mouth penetrated the fabric of his pants. The position she now maintained, the rush of adrenaline, provided an aphrodisiac effect that served to stimulate him beyond all bounds. Temptation to keep her there, to open his fly to provide relief, to see what she would do then, threatened his control until common sense took over and he released his hold on her.

She straightened and pushed the russet curls away from her face. "Well, that was rather interesting."

It could have been. Darin shifted in the seat and nodded toward the entry. "I assume that's the man your friend believed to be Birkenfeld."

Fiona glanced out the window as she slipped her shoes back on. "Wait a sec and I'll find out."

Before Darin could issue a protest, Fiona grabbed the keys, bounded from the car and met Mort at the door. She spoke with the bartender and stranger for a time before returning to the sedan, closing and locking the door behind her. "You're right. It's definitely not him. Poor guy. He thought gangsters were after him."

Darin yanked off the cap, tossed it aside and leaned his head back against the headrest. "Another dead end."

"For now, but I do know another place we can go, somewhere Mort suggested. Unless you're ready to call it quits."

Quit was a word absent from Darin's vocabulary. He would not give up even if tonight's search proved fruitless. He would continue on despite exhaustion and pain—and the woman who was proving to be a detriment to his determination.

He straightened and replaced his cap. "The night is still young, Fiona."

Her soft laugh took him aback. "Do you realize that's the first time you've called me by name? You're full of surprises tonight."

Darin experienced a sudden burst of energy, bolstered by the satisfaction in her green eyes and the promise in her smile. After surveying one more establishment, he would give up, at least for the evening. Then he would take her back to the apartment and expend some of his energy in more pleasant endeavors, if she readily agreed. If not, he would wait another day. But before he left, he would have her as surely as he would catch Roman Birkenfeld.

Fiona would have to agree with Mort—the Blue Moves Cabaret was several steps above the Frisky Kitty and a place that might be better suited for a doctor, even a demented one. The atmosphere was much more subdued, the music bluesy to match the moniker and the decor nicely appointed with cozy blue-velvet half-moon booths surrounding cloth-covered tables that faced the stage, an intricately carved bar spanning the back of the show room. An adjoining room housed several gaming tables and slots, but that area had been practically deserted when she and Scorpio checked it out.

Fiona figured the people who came here didn't come to gamble, although she was pleasantly surprised to see several couples, as well as groups of men. Much better for her and Scorpio to blend in. Just a twosome spending a late night on the town. A mismatched couple, but a couple all the same—at least that's the way it appeared as they sat in a corner out-of-the-way booth to peruse the patrons.

A busty blond waitress swayed to the table and addressed Scorpio, ignoring Fiona. "What can I get for you, sweetheart?"

''Coffee,'' Scorpio said then looked at Fiona. ''And for you?''

''Wine spritzer,'' Fiona barked out, incensed that the woman couldn't seem to keep her beady blue eyes off Scorpio.

The waitress left and returned quickly, giving Scorpio a wink and a smile as she set the coffee in front of him. When she served Fiona, she slapped the drink down at least a foot from Fiona's hand and didn't offer even a glance in her direction, or a cocktail napkin for that matter. Very bad form indeed. Fiona couldn't blame the harlot for admiring Scorpio, but she sure would like to tear that French maid apron off her waist and shove it into her collagen-enhanced mouth.

Scorpio paid for the drinks with a fifty-dollar bill and told blondie, ''Keep the change.''

The woman said thank you in a faux smoky voice, turned around, pretended to drop the money, then bent over to give Scorpio a bird's-eye view of her buttocks hanging out of the skimpy black shorts.

Fiona knew her kind well. Predator, plain and simple. She'd seen women like her come into the bar, looking for a rich catch with a bulging wallet and one foot in the hereafter. Scorpio was a prime catch, not only great looking but very alive and well. And obviously well-to-do if he could toss around tips equal to the national debt.

When blondie turned to apologize for her carelessness, Fiona played the role of jealous girlfriend by sending her a dirty look and laying a possessive palm on Scorpio's arm. ''No problem, *sweetie*. Now don't bother us again unless I give you a signal.''

Once the waitress left, Fiona took her hand away from Scorpio's arm although she really didn't want to. But he kept running hot and cold, and she just couldn't read him enough to keep tossing the hints, especially if he wasn't willing to receive them.

Lit only by a few bulbs lining the stage like a runway, the room was so dark Fiona still had trouble reading him. She could barely make out his features, yet she sensed he was hurting and his macho act was just that—an act. A display of toughness as well rehearsed as the woman's performance on-stage. At least this dancer could actually sing, and she was dressed, granted rather scantily in a very sheer red micromini dress cut down to there at her breasts, the bottom of the garment barely covering the matching panties she proudly displayed as she straddled a stool.

Several couples had taken to the dance floor, wrapped together like human pretzels, their passion palpable even in the darkness. Fiona focused on one particular pair who remained in place, clinging to each other like life rafts in a raging sea. She couldn't help but wonder if maybe they were married to other people, or if they were really that much in love.

Since when had she become such a skeptic? She still believed in love even if it had remained elusive to this point. Oh, she'd loved Paul in a way, but not enough to tune out the world to openly kiss and touch in public, not caring who might see or what they might think. Not enough to settle into a life that she hadn't wanted. And he hadn't wanted her enough to support her dreams.

Admittedly, that's what she longed for—real love and passion with a man who had no qualms about showing the world he cared about her. A man who held her in high esteem and considered life a full-time adventure.

As the stage lights went up, she glanced at Scorpio, sitting silent and stoic, his dark eyes inspecting the room instead of focusing on the woman who took a bow and left the stage to moderate applause. In her heart, Fiona knew he wasn't that man. He lived for the moment and the next mission, yet she suspected something drove him aside from wanderlust. She'd seen it in his eyes when she'd mentioned the name Tamra, a sadness that he hadn't been able to mask with his emotionless expression and casual tone. Maybe he'd been loved and left before, although for the life of her she couldn't imagine anyone breaking his heart. But then, stranger things had happened, and he did have a penchant for wearing mourning colors. Regardless, she would probably never know. After tonight he would set out on his own, leaving her behind.

Fiona decided then and there to make the best of their remaining time together, make a few memories to bring out on a rainy day when she again settled into celibacy until the right man came along. And she really believed that Scorpio could deposit some incredible reminiscences in the memory bank.

A few moments later the lights dimmed and an attractive couple walked onto the stage hand-in-hand. The woman wore a togalike black wrap that looked as if it might fall off in a strong wind, secured at the waist by a flimsy sash, her blond curls cascading down her back. The guy had blond hair, as well, and wore black tuxedo slacks, his gaping white shirt exposing a lean, tanned chest. Fiona decided they resembled life-size fashion dolls that should carry a disclaimer: Warning, not intended for children under the age of thirty.

A masculine voice from somewhere behind stage announced, "Ladies and gentleman, please welcome Sophia and Simon performing Night Moves." When they struck a dramatic tango pose, the crowd applauded and whistled. Fiona presumed this was a popular act, considering the noisy show of approval, so she settled back to find out what all the hullabaloo was about.

The rumblings of the crowd ceased as the couple began to move in time with the sultry instrumental. The action started slowly with a few synchronized dance steps until Sophia turned her back to Simon and stepped forward like a drama queen, as if to impede his advances. Simon obviously would have none of that and grabbed her hand, then pulled her against him.

It wasn't long before Fiona got the gist of what they were trying to convey when Simon's hands slid down Sophia's back then pulled up the toga to cup her bottom, basically bare save the black lace thong. Sophia, in turn, pushed Simon's shirt off his lean shoulders and it drifted to the stage in a heap of white cotton. Their moves became more suggestive, more sensual, giving a whole new meaning to the term "dirty danc-

ing.'' Yet Fiona couldn't deny that they were both very grace-
ful, and for the most part the performance was tasteful even
if highly suggestive.

Then why did she feel as if she were a voyeur peering into
someone's window from a perch on a rusty fire escape? Why
did she want to turn away yet couldn't turn away? And why
was she starting to feel so hot and bothered?

Simon soon divested Sophia of all her clothing except for
the strip of lace that barely qualified as panties. And when
Sophia yanked off Simon's tear-away pants, leaving him clad
in only a white G-string, Fiona physically jumped.

The low rumble of an abrupt laugh coming from beside her
caused her to tear her gaze from the dancers and level it on
Scorpio. She'd been so engrossed in the show, she'd almost
forgotten he was there. ''What's so funny?'' she asked.

He inclined his head toward her and whispered, ''Your reaction.''

She glared at him before homing back in on the couple
who might as well be reenacting a private bedroom video. ''It
just surprised me a little,'' she murmured, chagrined over her
obvious lack of sophistication.

Scorpio surprised her again by draping his arm across her
shoulder and pulling her close to his side. ''Is that all it does
to you?'' he asked in a voice as maddeningly sensual as the
dancers' movements.

''Yes.'' She sounded out of breath. Probably because she
was. And normal respiration wouldn't return soon, that much
she knew when Scorpio rested his palm on her thigh beneath
the table and drew lazy circles on the inside of her knee.

''I find it very artistic,'' Scorpio murmured. ''Erotic.''

So was Scorpio's touch, Fiona thought, as Simon, who had
fitted himself to his partner's back, took that moment to run
his hand down Sophia's torso, slowly, lower and lower until
his fingertips hovered just beneath the band of her thong. Then
he turned his back to the crowd, taking Sophia with him. They
swayed together, Sophia's arms coming back around Simon

where she raked her nails down his bare back, leaving no doubt she was in a sexual frenzy. Or at least pretending to be.

Fiona wasn't pretending. Every inch of her body was covered in heat, and a dull throb settled between her legs. She shifted in her seat, moving closer to Scorpio in the process. With a gentle hand, he inclined her head against his shoulder and brushed his warm lips across her temple. He slid his other hand upward, this time beneath her hem, rubbing his thumb back and forth, back and forth, on the inner part of her thigh, moving a little higher each time. The dancers were now stretched out on the floor, Simon braced above Sophia executing provocative push-ups, leaving no doubt what they were trying to mimic. And Fiona wished that she and Scorpio were doing the same thing—the real thing—right here and now, on the floor beneath the table. Only, she would insist on being on top.

Scorpio tipped her face up and touched his lips to hers, a chaste gesture contrasting with Fiona's less-than-innocent thoughts. She clamped her thighs together, trapping Scorpio's hand, but it didn't stop his random stroking. It didn't stop Fiona from wanting him to keep going.

"I could touch you and no one would know," he muttered.

"I would know," Fiona responded in a shaky voice.

"Yes, you definitely would."

"We can't," she said, her legs parting despite her protests, allowing Scorpio to brush his knuckles up her leg to the crease of her thigh then back down again.

"No one will see," he said. "They are too captivated by the show on stage."

Oh, how Fiona wanted to be so daring, uninhibited, adventuresome enough to just let it happen. But a woman sporting a platinum bouffant hairdo was sitting at the table not far from them, staring as if she suspected something naughty might be taking place. Her husband or boyfriend or whatever he might be, had his chin resting against his chest, sound asleep. No wonder she was looking for a vicarious thrill.

But Fiona couldn't let Scorpio do this. Not here. Not now.

She had to get her mind back on the reason why they were there, although she believed their attempts to find the fugitive would be futile tonight.

Fiona cast another quick look at the dancers. "We should go now since I don't think he's coming."

"If he's an expert lover, it will take longer."

"I meant Birkenfeld."

He worked his hand upward. "You're right. I greatly doubt he's going to show up here."

"Let's go then," she said on a breathy sigh.

"Not yet."

The music thrummed, rising to a loud crescendo, and so did Fiona's pulse, pounding in her ears while Scorpio's fingertip grazed the lace edging of her panties.

She should stop him, really she should. This was insane. Totally insane.

Just then Sophia and Simon left the stage to rousing applause and the house lights came up, signaling the show was over.

After Scorpio pulled his hand from beneath her skirt, Fiona slid from the booth and tugged at her hem. "Are you ready now?"

"That would be an accurate assessment."

"I meant are you ready to leave."

He wrapped his hands around the coffee cup. "Wouldn't you like to finish your drink first?"

She wanted him to finish what he'd started, someplace more private. "I already have, down to the last drop."

"Would you like another?"

Fiona frowned, totally confused over his reluctance. "No. I'm driving, remember? So come on."

"I need a few more minutes."

When she saw Scorpio twitch in the seat, much the same as she had, and his hand briefly disappear beneath the table, she suddenly realized exactly why he needed those moments. He'd been as turned on by the whole scene as she had been.

He was still turned on. So was Fiona. Her arousal wasn't so obvious. His would be.

She sent him a knowing smile. "Okay, while you take a few minutes, I'll go ask the bartender if he's seen Dr. B." She held out her hand. "Give me the picture."

He withdrew the photo from his jacket pocket. "I should be ready to leave upon your return."

Unable to resist, Fiona grinned and said, "I don't know, Scorpio. That might take longer than a few minutes."

"For your information, my leg is somewhat cramped from maintaining the same position for so long."

Fiona folded her arms across her middle and stared at him. "Okay. As soon as your *cramp* goes away, we can leave."

He smiled, slowly. "And I'm sure it will return as soon as we are alone."

Fiona headed toward the bar, shivering over what had almost happened, the suggestion in his voice. She was getting in too deep, losing her grip on reality. Having sex with him would probably only complicate matters, but it was too late to consider that now. Denying that she wanted him would be equivalent to refusing to acknowledge her dreams.

She intended to have him…and hang on to her heart in the process.

Five

Scorpio allowed Fiona to help him to the sedan, their arms wrapped securely around each other. He hadn't been totally lying when he'd said his ankle was troubling him, but that had not been his most critical discomfort. It still wasn't.

Seeing the seductive dancers, touching Fiona beneath the table, had brought him to the edge. He was hard, hot, sexually charged, and he needed relief. More important, he needed to find out if Fiona was serious about taking this further, taking this beyond the limits.

When they reached the car, he backed up against the passenger door she was trying to open for him and pulled her into his arms, capturing her gasp of surprise with his mouth, kissing her with urgency. Kissing her in the way that he'd wanted to in the club. He nipped at her lips, explored the edges of her teeth with his tongue, then thrust into the heat of her mouth, the way he would thrust into her body if the opportunity presented itself. He palmed her bottom and pulled her up against his erection, but that provided no respite. Only one thing would, but taking her in a parking lot against a sedan would not be advisable. When he let her go, she whimpered in protest.

"In the car," he demanded, then threw open the door, pulled her inside onto his lap then closed the door. The effort it had taken to move so quickly cost him in terms of his wounds, but he chose to ignore the pain.

After shifting Fiona around, bringing her legs to rest over the console and her back against the passenger window, she wrapped her arms about his shoulders and stared at him with an unwavering gaze. "I'm going to hurt your leg."

"You are not bothering my leg."

"Good. I wouldn't want to do that," she said, followed by a seductive smile.

"What do you want from me?"

She seemed surprised by the question. "Just some adventure, Scorpio."

"That is all you wish?"

"Yes." She looked away. "Of course."

Her hesitancy concerned Darin. "I live for the moment, Fiona. I do not intend to settle in one place or to settle down into a safe existence."

She leveled her green eyes on his. "Have I said I expect that from you?"

"No." Yet he could not help but believe that despite her talk of adventure, she would expect more than he could give.

She brushed a kiss over his jaw. "Why don't we dispense with conversation and go back to the apartment?"

"We will wait for a while."

She sighed. "Scorpio, we know Birkenfeld isn't coming here. The bartender's never seen him before. Besides, it's late. No telling where he is. I just don't see the point in staking out this place any longer."

He outlined the scoop neck of her shirt with one fingertip. "I do not recall mentioning a stakeout."

"Then just what do you have in mind?"

He slid his tongue along her lower lip. "Finishing what I

began in the club. What I wanted to do before you lost your nerve."

She inclined her head, allowing him full access to her delicate neck, which he plied with kisses. "I didn't lose my nerve. The lights came up."

"Perhaps you're not as daring as you believe yourself to be," he whispered with an added flick of his tongue on her earlobe.

"I took you into my house, didn't I? That was pretty darned daring considering I didn't know you."

He raised his head and flattened his palm against her chest then slid it up to her throat. "True." He circled his fingers around her neck. "I could have harmed you."

He searched for fear in her eyes yet he saw nothing but heat. "But you didn't, did you? And you won't hurt me now."

"How do you know?"

"Because I do know you better than you realize, Scorpio. I have you pegged as a good guy who's driven into dangerous situations by some major demons, probably because of something that's happened in your past. Something really terrible. Am I right?"

What had he told her last night in his drugged state? He dropped his hand from her throat. "I am driven by the search for justice." And his own guilt and grief.

She laid one palm on his chest, above his thrumming heart. "I'm not wrong about this. I have very good instincts. And my instincts are telling me now—" she wriggled her bottom against him "—that you definitely need something from me."

He did need her and want her, all of her. Wanted her with a fierceness that robbed him of control. Bending his head, he took her mouth again, deeper this time, more insistent as he palmed her breast, stroking his thumb back and forth across her rigid nipple. He slid his hand down and nudged her legs apart, seeking the damp heat between her thighs without formality. He wanted to touch her. *Needed* to touch her.

The panties proved to be a barrier, but only for a moment

as he tugged them down partway with a one-handed grasp as
Fiona lifted her hips, aiding him in his quest. She released a
soft sigh when he divined her slick flesh and stroked the small
bud that flourished with his touch. He pushed one finger inside her, then another, all the while keeping his mouth firmly
mated with hers. As she moved her hips in sync with his
caresses, he hardened more, painfully so, but that would not
stop him.

She shuddered and moaned and only then did Darin break
the kiss to watch her face. She was beautiful in the throes of
pleasure, her eyes hazy and her lips wet from his kiss. After
the spasms subsided, temptation to lower his head and give
her another climax nearly overrode his need to be inside her.

Later, he decided. When they were in a bed and he could
maneuver better. Where he could give every bit of himself,
as much as she was willing to take. All that he could offer
physically since he could offer nothing emotionally.

Yet when she looked up at him with satisfaction and
smiled, he felt something tug deep inside him, an odd longing
and unwelcome emotion. He pushed it away as he readjusted
her clothing.

"Wow," she said, still smiling.

"That is only the beginning."

"A really great start." She brought his head down and
kissed him again, quick and hard. "Now what do you have
planned for me next?"

He leaned over and whispered his plan in her ear, a common word in English that left no need for interpretation.

Her eyes went wide. "Well, that's one way to put it. A
little crude, but you won't get any argument from me."

"The word is not important," he told her. "It is how well
you interpret the word."

"How well do you do that, Scorpio?"

"Take me to your home and I will show you."

"What about Birkenfeld?"

"I will find him. Tomorrow."

* * *

From a car parked two spaces away, he watched the pair, furious to find that he hadn't mortally wounded Shakir after all, yet satisfied to know he had discovered the man's Achilles' heel—a woman. No surprise to Roman Birkenfeld. Women were responsible for most of the ills of the world.

He craned his neck to get a better view of the car illuminated by an overhead guard light. Although Shakir was vulnerable at the moment, he didn't trust that the tracker wouldn't be quick on the draw even with his girlfriend in his lap doing who knew what to him. Even if he couldn't exactly see what was going on, he did know they sure as hell weren't talking after that little display of groping he'd witnessed a few moments before. He did imagine what they were doing, in great detail, and that fed his fury, his own lust.

He really couldn't blame the bastard for wanting the redhead. She had the kind of body he wouldn't mind exploring himself, and maybe he would do that in the near future, payment for her tackling him in the alley and nearly getting him killed.

But he had more important things to consider aside from base urges, namely how to rid himself of the man who was determined to hunt him down like common prey. However, he would be forced to wait to exact his revenge. Wait until the time was right. Until he had the opportunity to dole out the punishment Shakir deserved. In the meantime he had to obtain the funds to get out of Vegas. Out of the country.

Right now he only had a knife and a stolen car in his possession and not nearly enough money…yet. But he would change his fortune and soon. He'd find some gullible woman to satisfy him in every way. Some rich bitch he could con. Vegas was full of them, and he knew just where to look.

And eventually he would punish Shakir. That wouldn't begin to even the score, but it would be enough for now. It had to be enough. He would kill the redhead, too, after he was done with her. While Shakir watched. Then he would kill the Arab, slowly and painfully.

For the first time in weeks, Roman Birkenfeld smiled.

* * *

Darin nudged Fiona inside the apartment, turned her around and pinned her against the closed door, then proceeded to kiss her. As badly as Fiona wanted him, wanted this, she pressed her palms against his chest and shoved him backward, nearly toppling him over due to his bad leg.

She raked her hair away from her face and fought to control her breathing around the suffocating feelings and mortification over what she'd just done. "I'm so sorry. Are you okay?"

He streaked a hand over his nape. "If you've changed your mind, you need only tell me."

She shook her head. "I haven't changed my mind. It's just that…"

As she searched for the right words, he studied her with his dark, compelling eyes. "What is it, Fiona?"

"Promise you won't think I'm a coward?"

"I would have a difficult time believing that of you."

She worked her bottom lip between her teeth, once, twice. "I'm claustrophobic. I don't like feeling trapped or being held down. That's why I fought so hard that night Birkenfeld had me on the ground in the alley. I was more afraid of suffocating than getting stabbed."

He frowned. "Why?"

This was going to sound so dumb, but Fiona figured he deserved an explanation. "When I was little, I was at my aunt Dina's house in Texas." Because her mother had taken off cross-country for the summer with a trucker, a detail she decided to leave out. "I was playing with my cousin, Howie, in the storm cellar. Howie thought it would be amusing to lock me in." The memories came back, scary memories of dank darkness. Her mother's sudden departure. The only time in her life she'd felt truly alone, until recently. "They didn't find me for several hours."

"You should have told me sooner."

"I'm telling you now. It's something I've tried to overcome but I haven't been able to so far. I know that makes me sound like such a wimp but—"

"I would never make light of a woman's fear."

Finally she looked at him, her arms wrapped tightly around her middle. "Thank you. Since you don't seem to be afraid of anything, I wasn't sure you'd understand."

"Everyone has fears."

Fiona waited for a long moment, thinking Scorpio might actually be ready to lower his guard. When he didn't speak, she asked, "What are you afraid of?"

He looked away. "I am afraid that my physical injuries might prevent me from doing our lovemaking justice."

"Somehow I don't think you're going to have any problem with that."

He smiled, a soft one that only enhanced the sheer beauty of his face. "Then you have not changed your mind?"

"No, as long as you understand how I feel about being held down."

He clasped her shoulders and turned her around, claiming the place where she had been, his back against the door, the equivalent of a gentleman laying his coat over a puddle for his lady fair, Fiona decided. Beneath that iron exterior of this breathtaking man lurked a true white knight, despite his dark clothing and eyes.

He pulled her closer but kept his hands loosely gripped around her waist. "Is this better for you?"

"Yes. Much better." They really didn't have to stand against the door. She had a nice bedroom with a comfy—albeit aged—double bed. But Fiona felt so safe, so secure in his arms, she really didn't care where they were at the moment.

Leaning into him, she braced her palms against his solid chest and he framed her face in his large hands. "I will relinquish all control to you, if that will make you feel more comfortable."

"Well now, that's an offer I can't refuse."

Cupping her breast, he thumbed her nipple. "Anything that I do that does not feel right to you, you may refuse. Anything you want, I'll see that you have it."

"Anything?"

"Yes."

Oh, yes. "First, I want to feel your hands on my bare skin."

Without hesitating, Scorpio yanked her shirt from the skirt's waistband, pulled it over her head, unfastened her bra and worked it away. He paused to trace a fingertip down the cleft of her breasts.

Fiona watched his movements, suddenly embarrassed over what he was seeing. Her freckles. "My dad used to say that I got those from swallowing a quarter and breaking out in pennies." Dumb, Fiona. Really, dumb.

He visually followed the path of his fingertip drawing circles around her nipples, first one, then the other. "I find them fascinating. I find you fascinating."

Overcome with a boldness she didn't know she possessed, Fiona pushed her pelvis against him, reveling in the fact he so was aroused. "Now take off your shirt."

After removing his jacket and the holster, he yanked off his tee in one smooth move, leaving his hair sensually stirred and revealing the planes of his wonderful chest. Fiona slid her palms across his collarbone, then grazed her hands down his sides, over his rib cage and back up again, streaking her thumbs across his nipples as he had hers. His skin was so hot and damp, almost unnaturally so. But then he was one hot guy.

Determined to continue, she brought her hands together in the middle of his bar-flat belly and paused where the stream of dark hair began below his navel.

Scorpio laid his palm over hers and pushed her right hand slowly down to his erection, holding it there. "Do you want this?" he asked in a rough whisper.

Fiona shivered. "I've wanted that all night."

"Then it is yours to take," he said, drawing her mouth to his in a high-impact kiss, a joining of lips, of tongues, of pure, hot pleasure.

He fondled her breast with one hand and slid the skirt's

back zipper down with the other. Fiona shimmied her hips until the garment fell at her feet in a pool of leather. Now all she wore was a pair of black panties and a full-body flush.

Scorpio broke the kiss to look her up and down while he lowered his own zipper and freed himself for Fiona's pleasure. And what undeniable pleasure it was, she thought as she stroked her finger up and down the length of him, eliciting Scorpio's groan before he whispered, "Your bed. Now."

Without a moment's hesitation, Fiona grabbed his hand and led him into her room, where Lottie had taken up residence in the middle of the pillows.

She pointed at the floor and said, "Down."

Scorpio came up behind her and circled his arms around her, radiating enough heat to fuel a volcano. "Do you want me on my hands and knees?"

She smiled back at him. "Not you, the dog. I'll put her in the kitchen."

Reluctantly leaving Scorpio's embrace, Fiona tugged the hound out of the room while muttering, "He's mine, girl-friend. Besides, you've been fixed." Once in the kitchen, she patted Lottie's head and gave her a treat. "Be a good girl. You've got plenty of food and water. I'll be back when I can." Hopefully not until morning, or at least after she got her fill of Scorpio.

Fiona walked back to the bedroom, arms folded across her bare breasts and pulled up short inside the door. Scorpio was stretched out on his back with his head bolstered by all three pillows, completely naked as if he didn't have a care in the world. He did have one heck of an erection, and Fiona had one heck of a case of the shakes.

Then she remembered something very important. "Scorpio, do you have anything…you know…condoms?"

"No. I had no reason to believe I would need any on this trip."

Fiona hadn't needed them for five years. "I don't have any, either. Maybe I should go to the store."

Scorpio sat up and braced his arms on bent knees, his head lowered. "I will go with you."

Somehow, having him put his clothes back on put a damper on the evening. But she wasn't stupid enough to let things progress without protection against pregnancy. And she wasn't too thrilled with the idea of traipsing to an all-night convenience store to buy a box knowing everyone would guess what was about to occur. If only she knew someone who might— "Wait. I have another idea." She grabbed for her robe and shrugged it on. "Let me make a call."

He glanced up at her. "You know of some place that delivers prophylactics?"

She laughed. "No, but that could be a very lucrative venture. 'Condoms on the Fly.'"

Scorpio didn't look that amused. In fact, he didn't look all that well. "Then who are you calling?"

"My neighbor. Peg, the one that took care of your cuts. It will only take a minute."

He dropped back on the bed and ran his hand down his belly, pausing immediately below his navel, sending shivers skittering up Fiona's spine. "I'll be waiting."

Fiona sprinted into the living room and took a seat on the sofa to dial Peg's number. After Peg delivered a sleepy, "Hello." Fiona said, "I need your help again."

Peg grumbled. "Don't tell me, your naked friend, Frank, got into another brawl."

"He's naked, but he hasn't been in a fight. Do you have any condoms?"

"What do you think I am, a midnight pharmacy? Besides, I haven't needed those things in years."

"Okay, I was just hoping that—"

"Wait a minute. I might be able to help. I don't want to be responsible for you getting pregnant or heaven only knows what else."

"I would be so grateful."

"And I'm sure so would your *friend,* Frank. I'll be there in a few minutes."

A short time later, Peg joined Fiona on the doorstep holding another brown bag. ''I have these left over from a bachelorette party I had for a nurse at work.''

After reaching into the bag, Fiona withdrew two foil packets and held them up to the porch light. '''Commando Condoms'? 'Ribbed for her ultimate pleasure'?''

Peg looked mighty proud, and sleepy. ''Yep. One's labeled Gargantuan Green, the other Promiscuous Pink. Sex in vivid color. I had some regular ones, but I didn't bring them since they were hanging on a tree.''

''A tree?''

''Actually, more like a few twigs in a red clay pot. We made a rubber tree for the centerpiece.''

Leave it to Peg. ''Not a great idea to use condoms impaled on a tree.''

''Exactly. These should do until you can buy some more in the morning.''

Fiona hoped that Scorpio wanted to do it twice. First, they had to do it once.

She dropped the packages back in the bag and groaned. ''I guess they'll have to do, but I can't even imagine Scorpio wearing a pink condom.''

''I thought his name was Frank.'' Peg's eyes went wild and wide. ''You mean you have a different guy in there? Way to go, Fiona!''

''No, it's still Frank. Scorpio's his last name.''

''Who cares what his name is or the color of condoms? Just get in there and make enough noise so I can hear you two doors down. Maybe that will wake up Walt.''

A hot blush crept up Fiona's neck and settled on her face. ''I guess that's the least I can do to show my undying gratitude.''

Peg headed away on her furry slippers and said over one shoulder, ''You can thank me later with the details.''

After closing the door behind her, Fiona went back into the bedroom to find Scorpio still reclining on the bed, only this time he was covered to his chin with a blanket, his eyes shut tight.

She tossed the bag onto the nightstand, perched on the mattress at his side and laid a hand on his forehead covered by perspiration.

"You're burning up," she said without bothering to hide her concern.

He opened his eyes, which looked glazed. "A direct result of your charms."

"You have a fever. You're shaking and you're pale. That has nothing to do with my charms." She stood and pointed at him. "Stay here. I'm calling Peg again."

He tried to sit but gave up after a single try. "That's not necessary. I only need to rest for an hour or so, then I will be fine."

"You're going to rest, all right. And I'm going to call Peg."

Pivoting on her heels, Fiona walked back into the living room and grabbed up the phone. Peg answered, sounding more than a little disgruntled.

"Peg, I—"

"Oh, good grief, Fiona! What is it now? Do I have to come over there and show you how to use them?"

"No, it's not that. Scorpio, he's got a fever."

"What's his temp?"

"I don't know. Lottie chewed up my digital thermometer when I left it out after I had the flu this past winter. I haven't replaced it yet. But he's very hot to the touch."

"Are you giving him the antibiotics?"

"Yes. Just like you prescribed."

"Have you checked the wound site?"

"Not tonight, but I can do that now."

Fiona walked back into the room, lifted the covers quietly so as not to disturb Scorpio, who appeared to be sleeping. "His thigh looks fine," she whispered.

"No joke, but what about the *cut* on his thigh?"

"I meant the cut," Fiona hissed, rousing Scorpio.

"And his ankle?" Peg asked.

"Just a sec." Fiona told him to turn over, which he did without even a muttered protest. She removed the wrap but left the bandage intact. "It's really red with streaks going up the back of his leg."

"Nothing nasty oozing from it?"

"Not that I can tell."

Peg sighed. "Fiona, he probably has the beginnings of an infection and the antibiotics I gave you might not be strong enough. Take him to the hospital."

"No hospitals," Scorpio said. "No doctors."

"You heard him, Peg."

"Yeah, I did. And it's just like a man. Give him some kind of analgesic for the fever and get him into the clinic first thing in the morning. We'll work him in. If he gets worse during the night, take him to the emergency room."

Fiona moved away from the bed, out of Scorpio's earshot. "I'm not sure he'll agree to go to the E.R. or the clinic."

"He better, otherwise he's only going to get worse. And if he's lucky, he'll be able to keep his foot. That is, if he doesn't die first."

Fiona shuddered at the thought. "Okay, I'll try to convince him."

"I'm sure you have your ways. I've never known a fever to stop a man—"

"I know, Peg. Thanks again for your help."

After Peg hung up, Fiona strode back into the bedroom to find Scorpio on his side, facing the window. She went into the bathroom, dressed in her plain cotton nightgown and returned with a glass of water and two aspirin. She sat on the edge of the bed and told him, "You need to take these pills."

"You intend to drug me again?" he said without opening his eyes.

"No. I intend to help you get rid of that fever."

Scorpio raised his head, took the pills and settled back onto the pillow. Fiona set the glass on the nightstand, checked her alarm then snapped off the light.

"Scoot over a little," she said, and took her place beside him, her back to his front, and pulled his arms around her.

"With you this close to me, I'm certain I'll recover soon," he said.

"You will go to sleep, and that's an order."

He rested his palm on her breast. "Only to sleep?"

Boy, Peg had the gender nailed. Despite his illness, he was still quite ready for action. She slid his hand down to her midriff and inched her bottom forward, away from all that marvelous maleness before she dispensed with the mother act and started acting like an overstimulated teenager. "Yes. Only to sleep. Haven't you ever done that, Scorpio? Only slept with a woman in your arms? You might actually enjoy it if you give it a chance."

She felt the immediate change in him, evident by his rigid frame. "It has been some time ago."

"Then there has been someone special in your life," Fiona offered as a statement of fact, not a question, because she knew she was right.

"Yes."

"Did she leave you?"

"I need to sleep now."

Fiona recognized she'd invaded a very sensitive part of Scorpio's soul, something she should avoid from now on. But she was so curious to know what had happened to this tough crusader and the woman he'd obviously loved. Maybe soon he would tell her a little more. Most likely he never would.

A long span of silence ensued until Scorpio said, "Thank you, Fiona. You've taken very good care of me."

"No problem. It's the least I could do since you saved my life." Saved her from a lonely, unexciting existence, at least temporarily.

His fingertips slid along her jaw as if he were memorizing her face. "I'm sorry we did not have the opportunity to continue."

"I guess we'll just have to put that on hold."

He tightened his arms around her and pulled her closer. "Perhaps in the morning. Or tomorrow night."

Fiona felt buoyed that at least he was planning on sticking around tomorrow. She would convince him to go to the doctor, make him a nice dinner and hopefully persuade him to let her continue in the search for Birkenfeld, but not until the following day. He needed time to recover. She couldn't stand the thought of something happening to her strong stranger.

In the meantime she would enjoy this night, these moments in his arms. And she would take them all to memory in preparation for his inevitable departure.

Darin reached out into the chasm, coming up empty-handed. The images were vague, surreal, but the arms around him seemed genuine, buffering him from the cold. A woman's arms. Tamra? No. Another woman who spoke to him in soothing tones, her voice comforting, calming. His limbs felt weighted, his eyes heavy, and he tried to force them open but could not. He tried to move but she held on, whispering he would be okay.

Another image assaulted him, the sum of his fears as he reached out for her hand that slipped away…. The devil incarnate had her in his clutches, vowing to destroy her. Darin would die for her so that she would live.

But not Tamra. Not this time.

"Fiona…"

The word drifted from his lips as he drifted back to sleep.

Six

Darin opened his eyes when he heard the incessant shrill. He glanced around the room and reached over to find nothing but a warm place where Fiona had been.

Picking up his cellular phone from the nightstand to halt the noise, he answered with an irritable, "Speak."

"Where the hell have you been?" Alex Kent sounded as incensed, if not more so.

"I've been searching for Birkenfeld as I've been assigned to do."

"Why the hell didn't you meet with the operative?"

Fiona appeared in the doorway while Darin presented an explanation to Kent. "I was already in pursuit before the agent arrived on scene. Unfortunately, Birkenfeld escaped before I could apprehend him."

"He got away again?"

Darin hated that fact as much as he hated Birkenfeld. "He was attacking a woman, wielding a knife. In the process of assisting her, I sustained some injuries. Minor flesh wounds."

"Minor flesh wounds?" Fiona said in a loud and somewhat incredulous tone.

Darin raised a hand to silence her. "I will continue my search tonight."

Kent's rough sigh filtered through the line. "Where are you now? The hotel has no record of your arrival."

"I never went to the hotel. I am staying with a friend." A woman who could have been his lover had it not been for the untimely fever.

"Is that the lady who answered the phone yesterday?"

"Yes, and she can be trusted. She's aiding me in my search by taking me to places Birkenfeld might be hiding. So far we have not been successful, and I'm concerned that he has fled the state."

"He's still there."

Darin sat up, his body feeling weak and wasted despite the positive news. "How do you know?"

"Because last night someone killed Larry Sutter in his hospital room."

"How is that possible when he was under guard?"

"Some guy posing as an orderly offed him, the con named Stokes who got away in Royal before we could capture him. They caught him, but not before he administered a lethal dose of morphine into Sutter. He claims he received the order from Birkenfeld and that Birkenfeld's still in Vegas."

"He has no other information?"

"No, but there's been a report that a man fitting Birkenfeld's description conned a wealthy woman out of a few thousand dollars last night, then knocked her around enough to put her in the hospital. If my hunches are correct, he'll gamble with the funds and try to earn enough to get out of the country."

Damn Birkenfeld. Damn him straight to the bowels of hell. "We are running out of time."

"Yeah, which is why you need to meet with the Bureau's operative. You can work together."

He glanced at Fiona. "That will not be necessary."

"Darin, dammit, you need—"

"To rectify my mistake."

"The Bureau will continue to be involved in the case. They're following leads as we speak."

"And we will see who gets to him first."

"You need to reconsider that. Birkenfeld is dangerous and desperate. You can't do this alone without risking your own life."

And he could be risking Fiona's life, as well, but he would consider that later. "I have come up against worse men. Birkenfeld is basically a coward. I will succeed this time, I assure you."

"I can't talk you out of this?"

"No."

"Then one more thing," Kent said. "He has to be disguised, since no one's found him yet."

"Regardless if he is disguised, I would know him," Darin said. He would never forget him, his fiendish eyes. "I'll be in touch when I have something to report."

"Darin—"

He clicked off the phone and tossed it onto the table, cutting off Kent's protests.

Fiona took a seat on the mattress beside him and ran a hand over his forehead. "You still have a fever."

"I'm well aware of that fact." Very much so. His muscles ached, and he couldn't seem to shake the chills, even though he could disregard his ailment long enough to persuade Fiona back into bed.

She stood before he could maneuver enough to pull her into his arms. "I'm going to help you get dressed and we're going to a nearby clinic. I'm not going to argue with you over this so you might as well—"

"All right."

She stood for a moment in shocked silence. "You mean you're not going to fight me on this?"

"No. Otherwise I will not be able to continue my pursuit."

"Well, hallelujah! Finally you're making some sense."

He could argue that point considering all the errors he had committed in terms of this mission, especially those that had involved his failure to resist her. He could not fail to protect her.

He would seek the treatment that would aid in his recovery, then he would leave her before he put her in more danger. And, regretfully, before they made love.

Roman Birkenfeld stood in the middle of the bedroom and admired his handiwork. Mind games were so amusing when played out to the fullest extent.

Damn, he was clever, much smarter than those down-home Texas do-gooders with overinflated egos who fancied themselves champions of justice. And Shakir... He rubbed his fake-bearded chin and allowed himself a laugh. How would he describe the Arab? A lone wolf son of a bitch who thought he had the upper hand in this round of cat-and-mouse when in reality he was no more than a pawn and a less-than-formidable opponent. The bastard and his redheaded whore were in for a surprise. A big surprise. If only he could stay and watch their reaction, like he'd watched them last night, but he wouldn't have that pleasure. He had somewhere to be. A place where he could get his gambling fix and expand his own borrowed fortune.

He laughed again, a shrill maniacal sound that echoed in the empty apartment, when he thought about the fifty-something, moneyed tourist ripe for the picking. The woman had been such an easy mark. Hell, he hadn't had to turn on the charm for more than five minutes at the blackjack table before he had her climbing all over him and slipping him her room key. Not very challenging, but productive, at least from a financial standpoint. What a fool she'd been, keeping all her cash in a hotel safe. And a bigger fool for laughing at him in her prissy hotel bed as if she really believed he cared whether he'd satisfied her or not. Laughed over his failed attempts at sex. Laughed like a hyena until he'd been forced to shut her up with his fist several times before her mockery quieted in his head.

He could still hear her laughing at him. Or was it Natalie Perez? They were all laughing. That bitch of a nurse, Marci, who'd spilled her guts to the authorities. Carrie Whelan, the woman he should've killed when he'd had the chance before the Old West rancher named Ryan showed up to rescue her. Laughing and pointing and taunting him over and over and over…

He clamped his hands over his ears to silence the din.

The sound of scraping against wood, not laughter, spun him around and drove him into the living room. He inclined his head and listened, recognizing the scratching came from behind a closed door at the far side of the room.

They'd found him! Those East Coast boys and their cronies had tracked him down. He shook his head, trying to clear the confusion. No. Shakir and the woman had returned. But how did they get past him?

The noise was deafening now…laughter and scratching and laughter and whining. They were trying to drive him mad, lower his guard. Sweat trickled beneath the cheap toupee and rolled down his forehead. His gaze shot to the front door and escape, then zipped back to the other door and the endless noise. He had to know if they were there. Had to know now, end the game, then he would leave. But not before he killed them all. Killed the noise.

Drawing the knife from the waistband of his slacks, he stalked toward the sound, prepared to do battle with whatever lurked behind the closed door.

Fiona glanced at Scorpio as she steered Darin's rental car through the complex's parking lot. She needed to pick up her own vehicle from the garage today, but at least this way she knew Darin wasn't going anywhere anytime soon, unless he went by foot, on a bad foot at that. But the doctor at the clinic had assured them both it would heal, no permanent damage done. The infection was mild and should clear up in a few days, if Scorpio cooperated.

"With the new antibiotics, you should be feeling much better soon," she said as she searched for an open parking space close to the apartment.

"I'm feeling better now. I am ready to continue the search."

Perturbed over his stubbornness, Fiona said nothing else while she claimed a spot two doors down, facing the street.

They both exited the car, and although Scorpio still walked with a limp, she didn't bother to help him. His body language alone told her "Hands off," very unlike their interlude last night when he'd made it very clear he wanted her. Those moments seemed far in the past. Fiona instinctively knew she wouldn't be able to reclaim them, because in a matter of hours, maybe minutes, he would be gone.

Before they arrived on the porch, Scorpio took her arm and turned her around, confirming her suspicions. He had "I'm leaving" written all over his face.

"Fiona, I appreciate what you've done for me. But I must—"

She laid a fingertip on his lips to stop the words she knew were coming but didn't want to hear. "I know. You have to go and do your duty. I guess it would be futile for me to try and convince you to stay. Or to let me help you."

He pulled her into his arms, right there in broad daylight as if they were lovers, comfortable with open intimacy. But Fiona recognized they weren't really lovers, and now they never would be.

"I've already put you in danger because of your affiliation with me," he said. "And after I leave, I would prefer you stay with someone for a few nights, perhaps Peg."

Fiona didn't want anyone's company except his. "Really, Scorpio. I'm going to be okay. If Birkenfeld knew where I lived, he would've been here by now."

"Possibly, or he could be waiting for me to leave to get to you."

"I doubt it. He wouldn't bother with some simple bartender nobody."

Scorpio smiled—a smile as brilliant as the sun hanging in the afternoon sky. "There's nothing simple about you, Fiona. And you're very beautiful. Birkenfeld would recognize that, and he most likely would recognize you as the woman who took him to the ground in the alley. For that reason, I will call my friend, Kent, to request a patrol in your neighborhood until Birkenfeld is found."

Fiona lowered her eyes because it was just too easy to get lost in his. "Okay, if you think that's necessary."

He lifted her chin, forcing her to look at him. "And he would also assume that you and I are more than friends, which would make you a target for his vengeance."

"But we're not more than friends." Fiona hated the disappointment in her voice. Hated that she was probably wearing her heart in her eyes.

"I consider you my friend," he said. "A very good friend. And if things were different. If I were..." He sighed.

"If you were what?"

"A different man. Someone who has not been hardened by all that he's seen."

She stood on her toes and kissed his stubbled cheek. "You have a soft spot, Scorpio. You just cover it up with that macho exterior. But I can see through it."

"You are a very intuitive woman, Fiona. I will not forget your kindness."

She would never forget him. If only they had succeeded in making memorable love last night. At least she could have given him that.

From her pocket Fiona withdrew the slate-blue marble, then opened Scorpio's hand and placed it in the well of his palm. "Here, take this. It was my dad's. Just a little something to remember me by. It's supposed to bring you luck."

He stared at the marble a moment before raising his eyes to hers. "This is not something you wish to keep?"

"You probably need it more than I do. At least until you

catch Birkenfeld. And if you're ever back in Vegas, you can return it to me personally.''

Fiona expected him to remind her that he wouldn't be returning. Instead, he kissed her deeply, deliberately, rousing all the feelings Fiona knew she should ignore but couldn't.

When they parted, he dropped his arms from around her. ''I can take you to retrieve your car on my way out.''

She shrugged, affecting nonchalance even though she really wanted to sit down on the sidewalk, throw a tantrum and have a good cry like a three-year-old. Instead, she smiled. ''That's okay. I'll have Lenny drop it off.''

He frowned. ''Lenny? Is he your boyfriend?''

She reveled in the fact he actually sounded seriously jealous. ''He's the guy down at the garage. I don't have a boyfriend, otherwise I wouldn't have been carrying on with you for the past few days.''

He nodded in an almost regal fashion. ''My apologies.''

They stood there for a few moments until he gestured toward the front door. ''I will retrieve my bag and be on my way.''

Resigned to his departure, Fiona slipped her key in the lock, puzzled by the sound of the radio blaring through the closed door. She hadn't turned the radio on, she was sure of it. Maybe she'd accidentally forgotten to turn off the alarm that morning.

That must be it, she decided as she pushed open the door and immediately strode into the bedroom to shut off some lively hip-hop tune that she might actually appreciate at a normal volume. Before she reached her destination, the icy clutches of fear stopped her progress.

Her pillows had been shredded into piles of feathers, the pair of charcoal sketches her cousin, Trish, had drawn of two historical homes in Shadowvale were hanging upside down. And her gorgeous mint-green sateen comforter had been desecrated with severe slashes that spelled out the single word ''Whore.''

''Damn him,'' Scorpio hissed from behind Fiona, startling

her. He grabbed her hand and yanked her beside him, keeping one arm wrapped around her as he withdrew his gun.

He pulled her through the room, using his body as a shield while he opened her closet, then her bathroom door to reveal that her decorative towels, too, had been shredded. At least they didn't find Birkenfeld lying in wait in the shower behind the glass door.

Then it hit her. Lottie. Her dog hadn't made a sound.

She'd left her locked in the kitchen. Left her defenseless and alone. And Fiona would kill Birkenfeld with her bare hands if he'd done anything to her precious baby.

"I need to see about Lottie," she whispered, her voice laced with an edge of hysteria, even though she tried desperately to hang on to her calm.

"In a moment." Darin moved back into the living room and muttered, "Stay close to me."

Fiona had no problem doing that since he had the gun and all she had was a belly full of butterflies and a feeling she might be sick, especially if they found Lottie— No. She had to believe her dog was safe. Had to believe she'd hidden or run away.

Scorpio checked the living-room closet and behind the furniture with agonizing slowness while Fiona's pulse pounded in her ears as he headed toward the closed kitchen door. He flattened against the wall, Fiona by his side still firmly in his grasp.

She held her breath as he opened the pocket door slowly where more chaos resided, her dinette chairs overturned, as well as the small table. The sliding glass doors opening up to the complex's courtyard had been shattered. And on the other side, Lottie sat on the porch among the debris, her paws crossed and her head cocked to one side. When she saw Fiona and Scorpio, she stood with her corkscrew tail wagging, something black hanging from her jowls.

"You're okay!" Fiona wrenched away from Scorpio and knelt to welcome Lottie into her arms, disregarding the shards of glass and the fact that Birkenfeld might be hiding in the nearby hedge.

"You are out in the open," Scorpio said from above her. "It is not safe."

She didn't care; her only concern at the moment was for her dog. She remained crouched to conduct a spot check over Lottie's coarse fur, finding nothing that would indicate she'd been injured.

As Fiona straightened, Lottie dropped the piece of fabric at her feet. She bent over, picked up the scrap and examined it. "It's the back pocket of a man's pants. Lottie must've torn it from Birkenfeld." She patted the dog's head and grinned. "Good girl, Carlotta. Smart girl, biting him in the butt." She faced Scorpio and handed him the pocket.

"Come back inside," he said.

Fiona followed behind him, patting Lottie on the head now and then as they made their way back into the living room, the only room that had been saved from destruction, or so it appeared. Then Fiona noticed the end table where the portrait of her mom and dad had been torn out of the frame, a slash across her mother's face.

"Sick bastard!" Fiona shouted. "I could kill him for this."

"And so could I," Scorpio muttered, venom in his tone. He picked up a small card lying next to the shattered frame.

Fiona clutched the picture to her chest and asked, "What is that?"

He studied it for a few moments then turned it over. "A hotel business card for a place called the Lost Springs Mine."

"The latest and greatest resort on the Strip. It's huge, or so I've been told. I've never been there. I hear it's home to lots of big spenders. A good place to—" her gaze snapped from the card to his eyes "—a good place to hide in plain sight."

"Exactly."

"Well, he should be featured on *Stupid Crook Tricks* considering he just left one whopper of a clue."

"Perhaps that was his intention."

"You mean like setting a trap?"

"Possibly. He wants revenge."

"And I'm guilty by association."

Scorpio studied her with dark, soulful eyes. "And I will never forgive myself for involving you in this."

Fiona shrugged. "Well, I said I wanted some adventure, didn't I?"

"At the expense of your life?"

"I know you won't let him hurt me."

"No. I will die first."

She swallowed around the boulder in her throat, unable to fathom why this man, this dark knight, would put his own life on the line for her, Fiona the bartender. He possessed more honor and courage than anyone she had ever met, male or female. And for that reason alone he would be so very easy to love.

While Fiona stood speechless, Scorpio tucked the card in his pants pocket, reholstered his gun and withdrew his cell phone.

"Thank God you're calling the police," she said.

"Not the police."

Fiona braced her hands on her hips. "Why not?"

Darin did not offer an explanation, not until he obtained the information he needed. After Kent answered, he said, "The hotel in which you resided while you were here last month with Stephanie, what was the name?"

"Lost Springs."

"And the hotel where the woman was beaten?"

"Same place. What the hell's going on there?"

He should tell Kent about the break-in, but if he did, his friend would have the place swarming with agents in a matter of moments. If Birkenfeld was still about, he would run. As it now stood, Darin suspected that the doctor saw this as some sort of sordid game. Eventually he would make the wrong move, and Darin would be there when that happened. "Call the hotel and make a reservation."

"Do you have a lead?"

"Only a hunch."

"He'd be a fool to go back there. The Feds have been checking it out, and hotel security has been put on notice. No one's seen him."

"True, and one would assume he would not return. Birkenfeld would recognize that."

"Then you're saying he's banking on no one believing he'll show up there again?"

"It's possible. I will conduct my own search."

"Okay, I'll call the hotel and reserve you a room."

A long silence ensued as if Kent wanted to say more about Darin's insistence on working alone. A few hours ago he would have gone to the hotel without company. But now Fiona was in serious danger. She couldn't remain at the apartment, and if she stayed with friends, that would mean putting more people in peril and leaving her an open target. Unless she accompanied him, Darin would not be able to protect her. And he had to protect her. He would not fail again.

"I'll call you after we arrive." He snapped off the phone before Kent could question him over his intimation that he wouldn't be by himself after all.

Darin turned to find Fiona staring at him, surprise etched in her expression. "We?"

"You are coming with me."

Who would have thought it?

Not Fiona. Little more than an hour ago, she'd believed she was saying goodbye to Scorpio for good. Instead she had packed a bag, sent a ticked-off Lottie to the kennel, and now they were sitting in front of the expansive five-star Lost Springs Mine Resort and Casino in the white rental sedan, sandwiched between two black limousines like the filling in a car cookie.

Scorpio was opening the trunk for a uniformed bellman to unload their luggage, which seemed totally unnecessary, since Scorpio had only the duffel and she had only a lone suitcase stuffed with enough clothing to get her by for three days, tops. Hopefully they would catch Birkenfeld before she ran out of undies although she supposed she could hand wash. She'd packed mostly jeans and T-shirts but had remembered to include the black leather skirt that seemed to have captured Scorpio's fancy the night before. And there was the matter of that little black nightie she'd never worn and the condoms she'd stuck in her toiletry case.

If a girl was going to be sequestered in a hotel room with a handsome hunk bent on coming to her rescue, she might as well be prepared for anything. According to Scorpio, she wasn't going to be allowed to leave the room while he searched for Birkenfeld. If luck prevailed, she would convince him otherwise. They were in this together. Even if she couldn't get her hands on Birkenfeld's neck, she could at least give him a good tongue lashing after he was caught. And if she happened to get close enough, she could give him two solid kicks in the groin—one for destroying her apartment and another for scaring her to death. Now she understood all too well the concept of feeling totally violated. She doubted she'd ever be able to live in the apartment again, even with the demented doctor behind bars.

Fiona slid out of the car and handed over her keys to the parking attendant after Scorpio insisted. She guessed his expense account allowed for such extravagances as valet parking and bellmen, although she wasn't sure that the Texas taxpayers would be too happy about it, if in fact he was a Texas cop, something he still hadn't confirmed. But she did know that he was one of the good guys, and that was all that mattered.

They entered the lobby, hand in hand, Scorpio assuming his usual on-guard persona, cap tipped low on his forehead as he visually studied the massive area that looked like something straight out of the turn of the century, all gold accents and red-carpeted floor with elaborate chandeliers and ornately carved furniture, right down to the cherrywood registration desk with the antique mirror hanging behind it.

Fiona genuinely doubted Birkenfeld would be standing by, ready to greet them with his nasty knife, considering all the people milling around. But he could be lurking somewhere, that much she knew, so she turned her back to the desk while Scorpio registered, keeping watch for anyone who might resemble the criminal.

"Your luggage will be delivered shortly, Mr. Scorpio," the desk clerk said in a very solicitous voice. "Please let me know if we can further assist you."

"We would prefer not to be disturbed after our luggage arrives."

Fiona turned to catch the desk clerk tugging at his old-time bow tie, his grin aimed at her. "I certainly understand. Just place the Do Not Disturb sign on the door and trip the privacy lock."

Here they were, in a high-dollar haven, and Fiona felt as if she were standing in a cheap motel, checking in as Mr. and Mrs. Anonymous to carry out an illicit affair. Ridiculous considering that unmarried people went to hotels all the time. She just hadn't been among them. Still, she found it darned exciting, especially the part about Scorpio not wanting to be disturbed. Yet she wouldn't allow herself to hope until she had him naked in bed. Until she had him in her arms, escaping all the ugliness and havoc wreaked on her world earlier that day.

After Scorpio obtained the room key, he took Fiona by the elbow and guided her across the lobby to the elevator.

Elevators. Fiona despised them. She'd spent most of her life avoiding them. They were too confining. Too frightening.

When the doors opened, her breath caught hard in her chest as panic set in. Scorpio entered the deserted car and held back the insistent doors for her to enter. "What are you waiting for?" he asked.

"I want to take the stairs," she said on a broken breath.

"We are staying on the twentieth floor."

She took a step back as if the mechanical monster was going to swallow her up. "I'll meet you at the room."

"You will not take the stairs unless I accompany you."

"You can't walk all that way on your bad foot."

"Precisely." A look of understanding passed over his face as he held out his hand. "The wall behind me is glass. You can see out. You will be safe with me."

The gentleness of his tone, her trust in him, sent her forward to take his hand and step into an elevator for the first time in years. Once inside, he turned her toward the glass and held her against him as the doors sighed closed and the car began to climb. "The hotel is very nice. Perhaps not as nice as the Plaza Athenee in Paris."

"You've been to Paris?" she asked in an unsettled voice.

"Yes. Several times."

She kept her focus on Scorpio's strong arms holding her close, not the whine of the elevator or the confinement she felt despite the transparent wall revealing the lobby growing smaller and smaller as they climbed higher and higher. "I haven't been out of the continental United States. I don't like airplanes."

He brushed a kiss over her cheek. "You are missing out on many adventures."

"I know. Maybe someday."

"We haven't had lunch. Are you hungry?"

She looked back and attempted a smile. "Maybe we could have a picnic in bed."

She half expected him to protest, to spout off about the mission. Instead, he simply returned her smile. "That could be very interesting."

"I'm sure it would be."

He lowered his mouth to hers—and the elevator chose that moment to stop and open, just when Fiona was beginning to relax and be ready for more of the good stuff.

Scorpio glanced over his shoulder at the open doors. "We have arrived."

"Looks like it." Fiona wondered if a time would come when they wouldn't have any interruptions, although she was more than happy to be off the elevator.

Again Scorpio took her by the hand and led her to the room. He slipped the card key into the lock and opened the door to the most massive, elegant suite Fiona had ever seen. A huge red-and-gold velvet-adorned room with windows that spanned the length of it, revealing the Vegas skyline. An opulent place that was beyond Fiona's wildest imaginings. But after she stepped inside, the door clicked behind her and she didn't have the opportunity to gawk when Scorpio pulled her around, back into his arms and kissed her thoroughly, completely, wonderfully.

He lifted her up and brought her legs around his waist, then walked into the room, backed up against the sofa and collapsed, bringing her into his lap.

Fiona laughed then, releasing the joy mixed with relief she felt so deeply in her soul. But her laughter died when she looked into his eyes and she saw desire there, so pure and hot and all for her.

"I should not want you this much," he said in a rough growl. "I should be concentrating on catching this criminal. But I cannot do that until I finish this."

She pulled off his cap and pushed his hair from his forehead, thankfully finding it cool to the touch, contrasting with the heat in his eyes. "I want you, too. But are you sure you're feeling okay?"

"I am feverish, but I do not have a temperature."

He tugged her T-shirt from her jeans and pulled it over her head, then unfastened and slipped her bra away. "I want to feel you in my mouth."

He'd no sooner said it than he did it, drawing her nipple between his warm lips, suckling with a steady pull that had her squirming from the heady sensations.

He grasped her hips and pressed down where she could experience his own desperate need, hardness and strength and power nestled between her thighs. She wanted all the barriers stripped away, wanted him inside her. Now.

Breaking the kiss, he set her aside on the sofa, then went to his knees before her. He effortlessly worked the fly on her jeans then pulled them down her legs in a rush. He took his time removing her blue panties, almost agonizingly so.

She considered asking again if he was feeling up to this and almost laughed at the absurdity of that notion as he slid his hands up her legs, parting them. Apparently making a place for him as he reached for his fly.

A loud rap came at the door, followed by a friendly voice announcing, "Luggage, Mr. Scorpio."

Scorpio muttered something unrecognizable as he stood, but Fiona didn't think he was telling the bellman to come in and join the party.

Fiona vaulted from the sofa, snatched her clothes and headed toward the door leading to what she presumed to be the bedroom.

When another knock sounded, louder this time, she turned to find Scorpio had yet to move. Instead, he stood in front of the sofa, his hands laced at his nape while he stared at the ceiling.

She clutched her clothes to her chest and said, "Are you going to get it?"

He dropped his hands and sent her a wicked smile. "I very much intend to, as soon as our unwelcome guest leaves."

Fiona felt the rise of a hot blush from her neck to her cheeks. "You should thank him. If he hadn't interrupted, we would've had to stop until he arrived with our luggage."

"And why is that?"

"Condoms, Scorpio. They're in my suitcase."

He fished through his pocket and pulled out two foil packages. "Not as colorful as the others, but still as effective."

Fiona's eyes went wide. "Where did you get those?"

"A gift from your friend, Peg."

"Then we didn't have to wait—"

"Until the luggage arrived? No."

Fiona could not believe the continued bad timing. "Get the door and then get thee to the bed."

"I'll be there soon."

"And, Scorpio."

"Yes."

"Give the bellman a tip. Tell him the next time he's heading to our room, he better call first. Otherwise, I might deck him.''

Scorpio laughed, a low sexy rumble that made her want to tell the intruder to go away so she could climb all over Scorpio where he now stood. ''I'm certain you would make good on that promise.''

She would make good on another promise to herself, too. She would remember that this little daytime diversion was just that—a diversion. She would not fall in love with him. Nope. No way. Never.

Then why did every beat of her heart tell her she should get out now, before it was too late?

Seven

Scorpio threw open the door, not bothering to hide his frustration or his extremely aroused state, something he could not very well disguise. Luckily the gentleman seemed oblivious to what he'd interrupted as he put the luggage inside the room, chatting incessantly about the hotel amenities and the in-room bar, complimentary of course considering they were residing in the governor's suite.

By the time the man completed his commentary and stood at the door, awaiting his reward, Scorpio almost told him of Fiona's threat. Instead, he handed the man a fifty-dollar bill and a look that said he was finished with all the pleasantries.

The man took the hint and left immediately. After the door closed, Scorpio tripped the security lock and cursed his powerlessness.

He should not be doing this, but he had no will to stop. Even his residual weakness from the fever could not stop him. His need for Fiona was so great that he stripped away his clothes on the way to the bedroom, taking with him only the condoms and the king of all erections.

He strode to the closed bedroom door and sucked in a deep breath, commanding composure he didn't remotely feel. But he had to remain composed, especially in light of Fiona's fears. He needed to be cautious so she wouldn't feel trapped or confined. Even though his body needed release, he would go slowly, carefully, earn her trust.

Entering the room, he was pleased to find her lying on the bed covered only by a sheet, a smile on her face. She didn't appear to be at all wary or reluctant, a good thing, since he possessed an almost frantic need to be inside her, something he must temper in order to do their lovemaking justice.

She tossed back the sheet without hesitation. "Climb in."

Darin set the condoms on the nightstand, and, just as he had one knee braced on the mattress, the phone began to ring. He chose to ignore it and slid into Fiona's arms to kiss and caress her while they faced each other. After the fifth ring, he released a curse and snatched the receiver from the cradle. "What!"

"Is that any way to greet a friend?"

Ryan Evans. Another Cattleman's Club member. Darin had not talked with him all that often since he'd become engaged to Carrie Whelan. "I presume you're calling about the mission."

"As a matter of fact, I am."

"Then tell me what you need."

Fiona ran a palm down Darin's bare thigh. "You know exactly what I need."

Darin clamped his hand over her mouth to silence her, but not before it was already too late.

"You got a woman in that room with you, Darin?" The amusement was apparent in Ryan's tone and in Fiona's expression.

Darin, however, was not amused or willing to be forthcoming with the truth. "A member of the housekeeping staff has arrived."

"Oh, yeah? Is she good with a vacuum?"

"Business, Ryan," Darin said, his patience a thin thread about to snap.

"Okay, business. Alex wanted me to call you because the information we've acquired came from the Bureau. Since you're so hell-bent on working by yourself, he has divided loyalties. That's why I'm telling you…to keep him out of the middle."

Darin sat up on the edge of the bed, his back to Fiona, who stroked her fingertip up and down his spine, threatening his attention. "What information?"

"A man fitting the description of Birkenfeld has been known to gamble at Lost Springs before on a regular basis, as recently as night before last, the same night the woman got beat up. One dealer commented that Birkenfeld claims his luck is better at Lost Springs than anywhere else. I know it's not much, but it could mean he might be back."

"I agree."

"So here's what we've come up with. In about twenty minutes or so, a tuxedo will be delivered to your room. We figure you can dress up and go down to the casino, check out the tables."

Darin despised the thought of wearing formal clothing, something he had not done in years. "Why is that attire necessary?"

"Lost Springs caters to high rollers. You'll blend in better with the crowd. Birkenfeld will spot you a mile away if you're wearing your usual black army gear. I'm not sure what you need to do with your hair to make you less recognizable, but I figure you'll come up with something."

Darin already had the kaffiyeh his cousin had insisted he bring with him. He made a mental note to thank Ben later. "I will handle it."

"Now, the dealer claims that the doctor comes in around six, stays for a couple of hours, then usually comes back after midnight to plunk down the big bucks. That's his usual habit, anyway. Who knows if he'll be back at all, but it's worth a shot. Gambling is his drug and he'll have to get a fix now that he has more stolen funds.''

''From the tourist he robbed?''

''Yeah. She made a positive ID from the mug shot. Seems she had a grand in the safe when the bastard beat her up. But that probably won't be enough for him to get where he needs to go.''

Darin consulted the bedside clock—5:30 p.m. Barely enough time to get a shower, get dressed and get downstairs. Ryan's call served to remind him that he should remain single-minded in his goal to apprehend Birkenfeld. He had lost sight of that because of his preoccupation with Fiona. He vowed to concentrate on his assignment and keep his hands off her. At least for the moment. ''My instincts tell me he will be back, if only to find me.''

''He knows you're there?''

Darin believed he could reveal more to Ryan since the rancher, who was somewhat a rebel himself, would understand. ''He left a clue behind in my friend's apartment, after he destroyed many of her belongings. I believe he blames me for his initial capture and now that he knows I'm searching for him, he wants revenge.''

''Good. Then he can walk into your trap.''

''Exactly.''

''Is this friend the woman Alex told us about? The one who answered your phone?''

''Yes.''

Ryan chuckled. ''And she works in housekeeping at the hotel? That's pretty damned convenient.''

''She is not an employee of the hotel.''

''Well, she must be pretty special if she's convinced you to take her along for the ride.''

''I only intend to protect her.'' His insistence sounded too defensive, and false.

''Good luck. Let us know how it goes.''

''I will.''

''And one more thing, Shakir.''

Darin braced for a warning about keeping his mind on the mission. "Yes?"

"I should've killed the son of a bitch after he kidnapped Carrie, when I had the chance. Now I'm relying on you to do whatever you have to do to stop this guy. So go get him."

"You can rest assured I will."

After hanging up the phone, Darin looked back at Fiona, who had turned on her side, one arm beneath the pillow, the sheet now fully covering her body. "You have to go somewhere, don't you?" Both her tone and expression revealed her disappointment.

He shifted and resisted the urge to kiss her, wishing he could discard all his responsibility and spend the rest of the evening endeavoring to make her feel good. "We have information that Birkenfeld could come here to gamble tonight, possibly in less than a half hour. I need to shower before they deliver the tuxedo."

She sat up and the sheet fell to reveal her bare breasts, bringing Darin's body back to life. "Tuxedo?"

"So that I will blend in with the crowd."

"I want to go with you."

He expected this. "No. You must remain here, out of harm's way."

"If Birkenfeld happens to find me here before you find him, then I'll still be in harm's way."

"Lock the door and stay near the phone. You can call me on my cell phone, and I will be here in a matter of moments if you need me."

"Yeah, sure. After you wait for an empty elevator or run up hundreds of stairs. By that time, I'll be dead."

Darin clasped her by the shoulders, propelled by a searing fear he could not explain. "Do not ever say that."

"Okay, okay. Lighten up." She ran her slender fingers up his arm in what should have been a gesture of reassurance, but to Darin there was something inherently sensual in the action. "I'll hit him over the head with the silver ice bucket if I have to. You just go ahead and do your thing while I stare at the ceiling and think about what might have happened if duty or the bellman hadn't called.''

He palmed her jaw and kissed her softly. "I will be imagining it, as well. And tonight we will finish this."

She lifted her shoulder in a shrug. "If you say so."

"I promise." A promise he hoped he could keep.

"Okay. Go take your shower now before I force you to change your mind and stay here with me." When Darin stood again, she sent a pointed look at his erection. "Take a really cold shower."

"That will not work."

She threw back the covers, exposing all of her enticing body. "I could take a shower with you."

"And I would definitely be late and quite possibly miss Birkenfeld. I will also need you to answer the door when the tuxedo arrives."

She came to her knees and grinned. "Do you want me to answer it like this?"

He couldn't stop his own smile or the fact that he grew harder before her eyes. "I only want you answering the door without your clothes if I am on the other side."

"That I can do."

Before he turned away from her, he took one last visual journey over her body, the pink-tinged nipples, the curve of her waist, the ginger shading between her thighs, subjecting himself to torture of the sweetest kind. "You'll find my wallet in the side pocket of the bag. Feel free to take some cash to tip the delivery person. You may charge to the room anything else you need. You only have to sign for it."

"Can I go downstairs and buy some souvenirs in the gift shop?"

"No. But you may have food delivered, and it's best you do that while I'm here."

She settled back on the bed and sighed. "Okay. I'll order some munchies and rent an in-room movie to keep me entertained. Maybe even a dirty one." She smiled again. "Then when you get back, I'll show you what I've learned."

Darin headed into the bathroom, no longer trusting his control. He only hoped that he could trust Fiona to stay in the room as she'd been instructed to do.

Fiona laid the tuxedo on the bed, grabbed several hundred dollar bills from Scorpio's wallet, stuffed them into her jeans pocket, then left the room before Scorpio came out of the bathroom and caught her disobeying.

She'd be damned if she was going to let him continue this chase without her. What better way to blend in than as a couple? But she did have one problem, nothing suitable to wear that would look nice next to his tuxedo, something she was about to remedy, as soon as she got on the elevator.

After punching the down button, she waited for an eternity for the car to heed her call. When it finally arrived, she gave herself a mental pep talk. She could do this without Scorpio. She could get on that moving torture chamber like a big girl and be no worse for the wear.

She kept telling herself that very thing for a good thirty seconds until the doors closed before she convinced her sneakers to move forward. Totally frustrated over her cowardice, she opted to take the stairs to the bottom floor and deal with her fear later. Right now she had to find a nice evening dress.

By the time Fiona reached the bottom level housing the boutiques, she was winded and a little weak, but that had more to do with thoughts of Scorpio and their afternoon interlude and the promise he'd made to finish it tonight.

She walked the corridors past several shops until a sassy, short, emerald-green dress on display behind the glass front of one store caught her attention. Perfect. Absolutely perfect.

She entered the boutique and approached a saleslady who wore lipstick the brightest shade of candy-apple red that Fiona had ever seen. "May I help you, honey?" the clerk asked, revealing a wide smile and a slash of lipstick across her incisors.

Fiona hooked a thumb over her shoulder. "The green dress in the window. I'd like to try it on."

The woman eyed her up and down. "You're what, about a size two?"

At least she hadn't asked if Fiona could afford it, which she couldn't. But Scorpio could. She'd just have to find a way to pay him back. "Actually, a four, depending on how well it accommodates my, uh—"

"Bust?"

"Yeah. It can be a problem."

"Honey, a lot of women would give their eyeteeth for your boobies. I'm sure the cut of the dress will make them look just lovely."

Boobies? Lovely? She'd settle for a good fit. "Well, I guess we'll see, then."

"I'll be back in a minute." Hot Lips disappeared in the back, then came out with the dress. "Let's get you settled in a fitting room and see how this works."

It couldn't have worked better, Fiona thought a few minutes later as she admired the cocktail dress in the trifold mirror outside the dressing room. The hem stopped about two inches above her knee, the satin clung to her curves, and the halter top fit her to perfection.

Not only would it complement Scorpio's tux, it could very well drive him to distraction considering it was low-cut and backless. And if the doctor didn't make an appearance tonight, then maybe this particular dress could help persuade Scorpio to go up to the room a little earlier than planned. A girl could hope.

"I'll take it," she told Hot Lips who stood nearby, appropriately oohing and aahing.

"A fine choice, honey. Will you need stockings and shoes?"

Oh, heck, she hadn't thought about that. She also hadn't thought about the time. After checking her watch, she said, "Yes, thigh-high stockings and heels, nothing too spiked. Do you have a house phone I could use?"

The clerk pointed toward the cashier counter. "Right there, honey. Size six shoes?"

Wrong again, Hot Lips. "Size eight. My feet are almost as big as my *boobies*."

The clerk threw back her head and released a screech of a laugh, drawing the attention and disdain of some silver-haired, bespectacled older woman inspecting the rack of satin pajamas. "Just come over and try them on after you make your call," Hot Lips said, and swayed away.

Fiona drew a deep breath and dialed the room number. Scorpio answered the phone within seconds, his hello anything but friendly.

"Look, before you get mad—"

"Where are you?"

Too late. He was already mad. Very mad. "That's what I'm trying to tell you. I'm downstairs, picking up a few things for the evening."

"Did I not say you are to remain in the room?"

"Yes, you did. But—"

"You are taking a huge risk."

Fiona knew all too well that she had a fight on her hands trying to convince him to let her join him. A battle she would definitely undertake—and win. "I promise you I'm fine, Scorpio." She looked around the room only to find the same woman still searching through racks of loungewear, totally disinterested in Fiona. "The coast is clear, so stop worrying. And don't leave before I tell you goodbye." Before she told him exactly what she had planned.

"I will wait until you return. But if you are not here in fifteen minutes, I will come looking for you."

"I'll be back by then."

After Scorpio hung up without saying goodbye, Fiona quickly tried on the pair of shoes the clerk had selected and paid for her purchase with nothing left to spare. Four hundred dollars would take a chunk out of her savings, but it would be well worth it—if Scorpio agreed to the strategy.

Restored by a rush of adrenaline, Fiona took the stairs

again, thinking she needed to start jogging during the week instead of just on weekends if she was going to engage in this kind of adventure. But after this was over, she would settle back into her old routine at the bar until she finished school in May. Then she would get a job, hopefully as an assistant manager at a trendy hotel, gain some experience and enough money to purchase her own place. She might have to start small, a bed and breakfast inn, but she'd do it. And maybe she would meet a man like Scorpio, only he would be willing to stick around.

Except she wasn't sure she would ever find someone like him. Someone who could so effectively take her breath away with just a look. Someone who could make love to her with skill and care. Someone who could stop her cold with deadly dark eyes, the way he did right then when she entered the hotel room and found him sitting on the sofa, scowling.

But gosh, he looked gorgeous in the white shirt that contrasted with his skin, the black tuxedo slacks that lent him an air of sophistication. He didn't have on a tie or jacket yet but she imagined he would look incredibly debonair once the ensemble was complete. If only she lived to see it.

"Where have you been?" he asked, not bothering to stand.

Fiona gripped the dress and bag to her chest. "At a boutique. I bought something to wear so I can go with you."

"Impossible."

She ventured forward a few steps. "Actually, it's very possible. I just have to take a quick shower and get dressed."

"You must remain here."

Fiona shifted the bag to one arm and propped a hand on her hip. "I'm going to do no such thing. We've been in this together as a team, and we should remain a team. Besides, what do you know about gambling?"

"I know enough."

"Enough? Which probably means not much. But I do know how to gamble, Scorpio." She'd been taking a terrific gamble from the moment she'd met him. "I can play blackjack and roulette. I can also play the role of girlfriend to your sugar daddy.''

''Birkenfeld could recognize you.''

''And he's not going to recognize you?''

''I intend to disguise myself.''

''With what? A mask? That's going to look a little obvious since it's not Halloween and this isn't New Orleans. Now if you wore an Elvis costume, I'd say that would work.''

''Trust me, I will make myself look quite different.''

''How?''

''You will have to wait and see.''

Fiona walked past him, heading to the bathroom. ''I'll see it as soon as I get dressed.''

''It is already past six. I need to go downstairs to see if Birkenfeld has arrived.''

She faced him and frowned. ''If he is here, which I kind of doubt he will be, don't you think he's going to stay a while?''

He stood. ''Regardless, you need to remain here while I search the premises.''

Fiona pulled out her last wild card. ''And I'll come looking for you. So what's it gonna be? You escorting me downstairs playing bodyguard? Or are you going to make me walk through the casino all by myself?''

He released a rough sigh. ''I am asking you to understand why I prefer you to stay here. You would be vulnerable to him.''

''And I would be vulnerable here, too, even more so, and that's if he's after me, which I don't think he is. But if he is, he's not going to try to kill me in a crowd. That would be utterly stupid. He might be the devil's clone, but he's not stupid.''

''I agree.'' He hesitated for a moment as if pondering her suggestions. Finally he said, ''I will allow you to come with me for a while. But if I sense you're in any danger, you must agree to return to the room.''

Fiona gave him a victorious smile. ''It's a deal.''

"Hurry."

"I'll be back in a bit. Thirty minutes, tops."

An hour later Darin was still waiting for Fiona to leave the bathroom. His impatience grew with every second that ticked off. His discomfort grew with each vision of her taking a shower, running her hands over slick flesh the way he'd wanted to do that afternoon with his mouth. And if he did not keep his mind on this assignment, he was in serious danger of putting them both in jeopardy.

At least by agreeing to let her come with him for a time, he could shelter her from harm—if Birkenfeld did not recognize them first.

On that thought, Darin walked to the bureau, opened the drawer and withdrew the kaffiyeh. He immediately thought of his brother, Raf, who still upheld the tradition at times, especially during business dealings. Raf, whose wife had died two years ago during an equestrian accident, the reason why he'd come to America to establish his horse breeding business. Although they were very different in many ways, they shared one thing in common—the loss of the women they'd loved. The Shakir curse had begun with the death of their own mother when they had been boys and continued into their adult lives when they'd become men.

However, Raf had covered his grief well, had even said he might marry again, where Darin had made it clear he would not consider it. But one truth remained, both had left their homeland behind to escape the memories.

Yet when Darin draped the kaffiyeh on his head and fitted the band to secure it, the memories came rushing back on a tide of emotion despite his effort to stop them.

Once more he was the prince, the young man who had reveled in his position, the power nobility had brought him. The second son of Sheikh Kareem Shakir, destined to share in the fortune made by his father and his father's father before him. The fiancé of Tamra Fayed, the only woman he had ever loved. Eight years ago that was all that had mattered, until

Tamra had been cut down in the prime of her life because of Darin's birthright. Now nothing seemed to matter.

Except for the woman in the adjacent room. Fiona was beginning to matter to him, more than she should. More than he should allow. He could never offer himself as freely to her as he had to Tamra. Never open himself to love again. The pain had been too great. Yet that pain had begun to subside in Fiona's presence, that much he would admit. When he was with her, he'd almost forgotten his failures. He'd also forgotten why he had come to Las Vegas in the first place—to capture a dangerous man before he could wreak more havoc on innocent women and children.

Darin must remember that tonight. Must remember why he was here and not what he wanted to do—stay in this room, close out the world and make long, hard love to Fiona. He must push those thoughts from his mind in order to succeed.

The door opened and Fiona stepped from the bathroom, shattering Darin's good intentions as he looked upon the woman who could very well be a living, breathing dream. She had pulled her hair up, revealing her delicate neck. The dress matched her eyes, hugged her body, made him sweat. Made him want to tear off the tuxedo, take off her clothes and bury himself inside her. He would request she leave on the high heels and stockings though....

Remember the mission, he silently scolded. Remember your purpose.

Her copper-painted lips curled into a smile as she pointed to the kaffiyeh. "That is a great disguise. You look like one of those Arabian sheikhs."

Little did she know, he was, something he would keep to himself for the time being. "You look very beautiful. The dress fits you as if it had been made for you."

She swept a hand down her side and over the curve of her hip. "Thanks. I thought it worked fairly well."

It worked on Darin's libido to extremes. He offered his hand for her to take when he greatly wanted to offer to divest her of the dress. "Shall we go now?"

She wrapped her slender fingers around his, her nails painted to match the color of her lips. "Yes, I believe we shall."

Darin led her through the suite and out the door, first pausing to look up and down the corridor before continuing on. Satisfied no one was lurking in the shadows, he guided Fiona to the elevators.

"Do we really have to get back in there?" she asked, her eyes filled with concern.

"I assumed you'd gotten over your fears after your recent journey."

"I took the stairs."

"And I prefer not to do that." The door opened and he nudged her inside. "Again, I will be here to help you."

Fiona took her place at the back of the elevator, facing the glass, while Darin once more circled his arms around her waist from behind, her frame stiffening as the elevator began its descent. The feel of the satin against his palms brought about visions of working the material up her thighs so he could touch her, make her forget her distress.

Before he could consider acting on that fantasy, they'd traveled no more than one floor before the doors opened again. Darin glanced over his shoulder to see a middle-aged couple dressed in evening wear entering the car. They sent Darin a polite smile and he nodded before peering out the glass as if taking in the view when he was only interested in taking in Fiona's scent. Taking her to bed.

The elevator stopped several more times until the car was jammed with people of all shapes and sizes, practically pressing Darin and Fiona against the transparent wall. He could hear her respiration increase even over the murmured conversations of the other occupants.

He bent and whispered in her ear, "Are you all right?"

"No," she said on a broken breath. "I have to get out of here."

When the car stopped on the tenth floor, Darin turned her around and guided her out of the elevator.

Once in the corridor, she collapsed against the wall, trembling. "I'm sorry I'm such a coward, but—"

He leaned over and brushed a kiss across her lips. "You need not apologize. We can take the stairs the rest of the way."

She looked at him with gratitude. "Thanks for understanding. I promise I'll be brave when we come back up."

"And I promise I will keep you safe. If you do as you're told."

A smile broke through her anguish. "That depends on what you're telling me to do. If it involves activities between the sheets, then I'm all for instructions."

"I'm referring to our search for Birkenfeld."

"That's too bad. I was hoping maybe you might put that off for a while so we can go back to the room and finish what we started this afternoon."

"Perhaps we will do that later."

Her grin deepened. "Oh, good. As long as I can be on top."

Muttering a mild oath, Darin took her by the hand and led her to the stairway before he lost his dignity. Before he disregarded good sense and made love to her against the wall.

The first three floors were not that troublesome to his ankle, but before he reached the final landing, his wound throbbed. Fiona glanced at him with concern and stopped. "I am so stupid. I didn't even think about your foot."

"It is fine," he said, gritting his teeth against the pain. "We're almost there."

When they reached the lobby, he pulled Fiona close to his side as they crossed the red-carpeted walkway leading to the casino, working their way through the crush of people heading in the same direction. His limp was more pronounced now, and he hated being so obvious.

As he kept keen eyes on his surroundings, Darin told Fiona, "You must stay close to me. If you have to leave the floor, I will go with you."

"What if I need to go to the ladies' room?"

"I will follow you and wait outside."

"Nothing like being held prisoner in a hotel."

He stopped and turned her to face him, his hands circling her bare arms. "I must have your promise now that you will not take any chances. Otherwise, I will carry you back to the room over my shoulder."

She had the audacity to grin. "Maybe I should misbehave just to see if you'll really do it."

He narrowed his eyes. "I am warning you, Fiona."

"And I'm kidding, Scorpio. You can barely carry your own weight on your foot." She moved to his side and linked her arm with his. "Now let's go see if we can catch the very evil Dr. B."

Exactly why they were here, Darin reminded himself as they once more headed toward the casino. But with every cautious breath he drew, with every painful step he took, he considered turning around and scrapping this quest for a few moments in Fiona's arms.

He was dangerously close to tossing wisdom to the wind, and that made him prone to making mistakes, primed him for more failures. From this point forward he would remain in control or risk losing this game and, in doing so, possibly losing Fiona in the process—a woman who was coming to mean far too much to him.

Again his past was threatening to return and so were the emotions he'd kept carefully hidden from the world, and from himself. He would push them away, vanquish them once and for all. Otherwise they could be the death of him. And Fiona.

Eight

At half past nine, Fiona had grown tired of walking the various levels of the casino. So far, not one person they'd seen even remotely resembled Birkenfeld. She suspected the criminal was long gone after having left his calling card in her apartment and scaring the willies out of her. If he did happen to show up, he would be a fool, since he was bound to know Scorpio would be looking for him. And probably so were all the security guards swarming the area, more than she'd seen in a casino before.

When a raucous crowd at a nearby craps table drew her attention, she stopped to take in all the commotion. Scorpio tugged on her hand and she tugged back, halting his progress. "Just a minute. I want to watch for a while."

"We must keep moving," he said.

She sent him a cynical look. "You really ought to get off your foot, especially since you refused to wear that lovely blue shoe they provided."

"I am mobile enough without it."

Darned headstrong man. "Tell you what. I'll stay right here in this group and you keep looking around. Your foot might be fine, but my feet are killing me."

"I've told you what I need you to do."

"And I've told you what I need you to do. Since you don't plan to do that anytime soon, the least you can allow me is a little opportunity to have some fun."

"I would not feel comfortable leaving you alone."

She nodded toward two security guards standing nearby. "I'm not alone. Those guys are only a shout away."

After hesitating for a moment, he finally said, "Do you promise you will not leave here until I return?"

She tugged her hand out of his grasp and raised it in oath. "I hereby swear not to leave the premises." She dropped her hand and sent him a smile. "And bring me something to drink, will you? A white wine."

He frowned. "If I have the opportunity. I will return after I check the upper floor again." He turned away then faced her again. "Do not leave. If you feel threatened, find a guard."

"Okay, I will."

After Scorpio walked away, Fiona inched closer to the head of the table where a bearded middle-aged guy in an expensive silver suit, his semipompadour cemented in place by probably a can of hairspray, awaited his turn to roll the dice. He glanced at Fiona and sent her a smarmy smile. "Hello, little lady. Are you feeling lucky tonight?"

She was hoping to get lucky tonight, but not with this guy. "Reasonably so."

He elbowed the man next to him over a bit and offered Fiona the space. "Come here and roll the dice for me, baby. I could use some luck."

He could use some gum, Fiona thought as she stood beside him, overwhelmed by his liquor-laden breath and overpowering cologne. She selected two dice from the dealer, but she wasn't too thrilled when the pompadour guy blew on her closed fist. At least he wasn't blowing in her ear...yet.

While the participants gathered round the table and stared at her expectantly, Fiona rolled the dice, landing a three and seven and earning cheers.

"What's your name, babe?" the gambler asked as the dealer settled the bets.

"Fee-Fee," she said, thinking that was better than babe.

His grin was as slick as his hair. "Oh, yeah? My grandma had a poodle named Fee-Fee once. A real good lap dog." He wriggled his eyebrows and held out his hand. "Nice to meet you, Fee-Fee. I'm Gary."

"Nice to meet you, too, Gary." A whopper of a lie. If she hadn't been so bored, she would definitely turn tail and run far, far away from him.

Gary placed a huge bet on the table and said, "Now you do your best to make me a richer man, baby."

She would do her best to avoid his leer and concentrate on her dice-rolling duty. This time she rolled another seven and found herself totally caught up in the enthusiasm of the game. With each roll of the dice she became more popular, with the crowd betting on her luck, although she didn't appreciate Gary who had managed to move closer to her. She ignored his proximity, tried to ignore his stubby hand occasionally grazing her bare back. So far his actions were relatively harmless, until his palm landed on her butt.

"Remove your hand from her immediately."

Fiona's gaze snapped to Scorpio's menacing stare. How long had he been standing there, watching her?

Gary looked over his shoulder at Scorpio who stood at least a head taller than the gambler. "And who are you to tell me what I should do?"

"Her husband."

Her husband? Did Fiona actually hear him say that?

Gary dropped his hand from her derriere and asked, "Do you know this guy?"

Fiona laid the dice down and backed away from the table. "Yes. I'm with him."

Gary gave Scorpio an incredulous look. "Listen, man, I

wouldn't leave this lady alone for a minute. She's the best-looking gal in this place tonight."

"And she is mine," Scorpio said, his tone as fierce as his eyes.

Fiona grabbed Scorpio's hand now balled in a fist. "Come on, dear. I think I hear the slot machines calling me."

She shouldered her way toward the cashier's cage in the corner, pulling him along behind her. "I'm guessing you didn't find Birkenfeld," she said after she faced him again. "Otherwise, you wouldn't have interrupted my good time by spouting all that macho 'she's mine' garbage."

He looked no less angry. "No, I did not find Birkenfeld. I did find you fraternizing with a man who had less than honorable intentions, while a murderer could very well be stalking you."

Fiona rolled her eyes to the ornate chandelier above them. "Face it, Scorpio. Birkenfeld isn't here and he's probably not coming. That guy at the table was totally harmless and, granted, moderately disgusting, but I needed something to occupy my time while you were out conducting a futile search."

"That is why we are here, Fiona. To search. And since that is not holding your interest, I will escort you back to the room so I can continue without having to concern myself with your activities."

Fiona's mouth dropped open. "Concern yourself with my activities?" She laid a hand on her chest. "Oh, please. I stopped needing a keeper about fifteen years ago." In fact, she'd grown up being her mother's keeper. Grown up too fast.

Incensed over Scorpio's belief she couldn't take care of herself, Fiona spun on her uncomfortable heels and headed toward the rest room.

"Where are you going?" Scorpio said after catching up to her.

"Somewhere you can't go," she replied, pushing open the bathroom door in order to calm her anger and catch her breath.

Once inside, she braced her hands on the red-and-gold marble vanity and stared at her face in the faux antique mirror.

Her lipstick was practically gone and her hair had started to unravel from the updo. She might look disheveled and annoyed, but she didn't look that crazy. But obviously she was totally insane, out of touch with reality. She should know better than to hook up with a man like Scorpio or Darin or whatever his name was. A demanding, serious man who obviously expected his women to *behave* like good little girls. A man who delighted in rescuing her from all the drunk Don Juans of the world. A man who had the absolute nerve…to walk into a women's rest room.

Fiona spun from the mirror and glared at him. "What are you doing in here?"

He tripped the bolt on the door behind him. "Making certain you do not run away before we discuss your insistence on ignoring the rules and safety."

She made a sweeping gesture around the lounge. "And how am I going to get out of here? Through the ventilation system?"

With two long strides he was standing before her, tall and dark and imposing. He smelled like a summer night and looked like an all-expense-paid trip to Valhalla. "I was not willing to take the risk, considering you are very resourceful."

The vanity's ledge bit into Fiona's bottom as she tried to back away from all that charisma before she forgot her anger. "We can take this outside before someone comes out of the stall and calls security."

He braced his palms on either side of her, leaving only a small space between them. "Are you certain we're not alone?"

Fiona ducked under his arm, left the area and slammed doors back with the force of her frustration to find the ten or so stalls unoccupied. She strode into the lounge to discover Scorpio leaning back against the vanity where she had been. He looked totally out of place among the feminine accoutrements but much too handsome to ignore. "We're alone now," she said. "But someone's bound to want to get in here."

He crossed his arms over his broad chest as if they had all

the time in the world. "Tell me, did you find that man at the table to your liking?"

She exhaled an impatient sigh. "Not that again."

"He seemed quite taken with you."

"He only wanted someone to toss his dice for luck."

"He wanted to toss you into his bed."

She shrugged. "So what? I wasn't going to go anywhere with him."

"I am pleased to hear that. I doubt he could adequately satisfy you."

Oh, but Scorpio could. Fiona was well aware of that. And darned, she wanted him to satisfy her and soon—ridiculous, considering she should be irate. "We can talk about this in the suite."

"I do not want to talk any longer."

Surely he didn't mean… "Then what do you have in mind?"

"Come here and I will show you."

Did she dare do that? Did she really dare answer the plea in his dark eyes, her own desire for him, in a public rest room no less?

True, she wanted adventure. And she wanted him. Oh, did she want him. That propelled her forward into his open arms to accept his kiss and his soft abrading tongue between her parted lips.

He broke the kiss and whispered, "I admit, I could not stand to see that man's hands on you, even if I have no claim on you."

She leaned back and looked into his eyes. "Believe me, you don't have anything to worry about. The only hands I want on me are yours."

He slid a slow fingertip across her collarbone then down the valley between her breasts. "And I want to put my hands on you. My mouth on you. Everywhere."

He reached around her neck and tugged the clasp open, allowing the strips of green satin forming the halter to fall to her waist, exposing her bare breasts.

"We can't do this here," she murmured without much conviction.

He dropped his hands to his sides, challenge in his infinitely mysterious eyes. "Then redo your dress and we will leave."

She lifted her chin. "You opened it, you redo it."

His eyes burned hot, burned Fiona right to the feminine core. "No."

"You're stubborn."

"True, I am. When I want something badly enough. And I want you. Badly."

Her pulse picked up speed. "Here?"

"Now."

"That's crazy." Fiona reached down to pull the bodice back up, really that's what she intended to do. But instead of raising the top back into place, she lifted her breasts and offered them to him. He bent his head and drew one nipple into his mouth, flicking his tongue back and forth over her rigid flesh while he kneaded her bottom.

She pulled the cloth from his head and tossed it aside so she could work her hands through his silky dark hair. He continued to finesse her breasts with his lips, the gentle scrape of his teeth, the steady pull of his mouth.

In five more minutes Fiona would bet all the coins in Vegas that she wasn't going to be able to stop him. She didn't want to stop him, not even when she heard the rasp of his zipper. She had to know how it would feel to make love with him in wild ways, in a forbidden place. Even here. Even now.

"Touch me," he murmured. "I want to feel your hands on me."

Reaching between them, Fiona slipped her palm inside his open fly and appraised the territory with curiosity and care, exploring the varying textures and learning exactly which were sensitive just by listening to Scorpio's breathing, or lack thereof, when she hit the right spot. This totally wicked foreplay made her body boneless and her breathing as irregular as his. Made her hot as a bonfire and weak with a need that only he could satisfy. She was only faintly aware of the impatient knocks at the door until the handle jiggled and a loud voice called, "Housekeeping. Is anyone in there?"

Fiona wanted to shout, "Go away!" but thought better of it. The last thing they needed was to create a scene and get caught in a compromising position.

After pulling her hand away, she said, "Let's take this upstairs before they call in the guards."

"I could pay them to leave," Scorpio murmured as he fondled her breasts with both hands, his eyes locked on to hers.

Gathering all the strength she could muster, Fiona took a step back and redid her dress. "We have a perfectly good bed waiting for us. Unless you want to continue this pointless search for Birkenfeld."

Pushing away from the counter, he folded the cloth in precise creases and tucked it and the gold band in the inside jacket pocket. He then circled his arms around her without bothering to refasten his fly. "I will resume the search later, when I can concentrate." He pressed her palm against his erection. "After I take care of this."

"The best idea you've had all night." She raised his zipper. "But not here."

Before Fiona changed her mind and decided to ignore the chorus of protesting feminine voices outside the door, she disengaged the lock and walked out with Scorpio trailing behind her. She ignored the furtive glances, the nervous giggles as they strode past the line of fidgeting females, until she glanced to her right and saw the same woman from the boutique leering as if Fiona was the devil's spawn. The uptight granny reminded Fiona of her aunt Oralene who hadn't been happy unless she was sitting in judgment of someone. If Fiona wasn't in such a hurry to get Scorpio alone, she'd stop and tell the lady to get a chin wax and an attitude adjustment.

Scorpio came to Fiona's side and entwined his fingers with hers as they maneuvered through the masses coming into the casinos. Fiona felt her heart beat in a crazy cadence. She was finally going to have what she needed, Scorpio's full attention. But when they reached the elevator, fear replaced her anticipation, especially when she noticed all the people crowding into the car.

As if sensing her trepidation, Scorpio pulled her against his side. "We will wait for the next one to arrive."

By the time that happened, another group had gathered, smaller this time but too many for Fiona's comfort. Scorpio held the doors open and she moved inside on noodle legs. But as the first occupants started to enter, Scorpio held up a hand to stop them. "My wife is very nervous on elevators. I should warn you that she sometimes loses control. You're welcome to join us if you can tolerate her screams."

They simultaneously backed off, and Scorpio allowed the doors to close.

Fiona hugged her arms to her middle and drew in a deep breath as the elevator started its climb. "Was that really necessary? I might hyperventilate, but I have no intention of screaming."

"Perhaps you will at that."

Fiona noted the heat in his eyes as he flipped a switch on the silver panel. The car came to an abrupt halt between the fifth and sixth floors and so did Fiona's heart.

"What are you doing?" she asked when she could finally speak.

"Turn around and look out the glass."

"I can't move." Her voice sounding weak and shaky, complementing her legs. "I have to get out of here. Now."

"Not yet."

She closed her eyes and exhaled slowly. "Look, if this is your idea of therapy, trap Fiona in an elevator and force her to face her fears, it's not going to work."

"We will not be here long, I assure you," he said as he took her by the shoulders and turned her around. "In approximately five minutes, an alarm will begin to sound if the elevator does not move."

Alarms sounded in Fiona's brain even when Scorpio slipped one arm around her from behind and pulled her against him. "Try to relax," he whispered as he ran one palm down the back of her thigh then up again, taking her dress with him, exposing her bottom to the cool draft of air filtering into the elevator and the heat of his hand.

"What are you doing now?" she asked, her voice no less shaky.

"I am giving you good memories of elevators." He kissed her neck. "I am going to give you something to make you forget your fears. Something good to make you scream."

"You're going to get us arrested," she said as he slid his hand beneath her panties to work his magic on bare skin.

"No one will see us," he said in a low voice. "Not even when I do this."

Fiona gasped when he cupped his palm between her thighs and skated one finger over her flesh, back and forth in a tantalizing rhythm. She braced her palms on the glass to keep from wilting onto the floor. His insistent touch, his ardent stroking stoked the fire and blocked all her fears. She was entirely immersed in the sensations, wet from his caress and the fact that they were in an elevator with a glass wall and anyone who had a mind could look up and know by her face what was happening. Know because Scorpio's other hand came up to weigh her breast, his thumb passing over her nipple in sync with his finger thrusting deep inside her.

She leaned back against him, dizzy from the rapidly approaching climax, fearing she might slide to the ground. He held fast to her but even when the series of endless spasms began, he didn't let up. And when the alarm sounded, Fiona shuddered and released a long moan that bordered on a scream.

The elevator began to move again, but she truly didn't care. She only cared about Scorpio and what he had done to her. She turned into his arms and kissed him, knowing that in a short time, he would be hers completely, at least for tonight.

From the lobby below, a bespectacled, silver-haired woman watched the elevator's ascent. To most observers, she appeared to be any tourist taking a break from the hustle and bustle of the casino craze. To most passersby, she could be someone's cookie-baking, blanket-knitting mother up from Florida on a summer junket to Vegas.

But she wasn't a woman at all. She was a desperate man caught in the throes of madness, bent on revenge, filled with a hatred that knew no bounds.

A clever man who had no job, no money to speak of and no pride. A man who a year ago would never have donned a shapeless black dress and ugly sensible shoes along with a wig that felt like a vise covering his pounding head.

He couldn't stop the noise racing through his brain, the voices that taunted him, voices of the people who thought they were smarter than him. In reality, they were stupid and careless and he would find them soon. Shakir and his red-headed lover, Natalie. No, not Natalie. But they were one and the same. Maybe he couldn't recall her name, but he knew what she was and what she deserved. In a matter of hours he would watch her suffer, and he would watch her die along with Shakir.

They could go to their high-dollar suite and screw like rabbits and he would be waiting for them when they came back downstairs, and they would return because Shakir wouldn't give up that easily. And Roman Birkenfeld, once esteemed doctor, would be waiting with glee to slit Shakir's aristocratic throat.

Never before had a woman held so much power over Darin Shakir. Never before had he wanted someone so fervently that he would neglect his responsibilities. The mission no longer mattered once he had Fiona in the suite, divesting her of the dress between kisses as they made their way into the bedroom. Once there, he made quick work of the jacket and tie, tossing them aside, then struggled out of the confining shoes and socks. Fiona stood silently watching, clad only in sheer lace panties, stockings that came to her thighs and high heels.

Wearing only his slacks, he sat on the edge of the mattress to look his fill and to reclaim his control. After a long visual journey over her body, his gaze came to rest on her tentative expression, fearing that she would change her mind, knowing that honor bound him to respect her decision, whatever that decision might be.

He clasped her hands and pulled her forward between his legs. "What is it?"

She worked her bottom lip between her teeth. "I've only done this a couple of times with one man."

Darin was somewhat surprised by the revelation, yet he would endeavor to put her mind at ease. "It is not something you easily forget."

She lowered her eyes to their joined hands. "Unless it was forgettable."

"Did the man you were with not treat you well?"

"Let's just say he didn't appreciate my...problem."

Darin's understanding began to dawn. "Your fear of confinement, you mean."

"Yes. I never told him about it. He just thought I wasn't all that interested in lovemaking."

He reached up and lifted her chin, seeking her eyes. "I will make certain that you experience pleasure. That our time, together—" he entwined their fingers, symbolizing the joining they would soon undertake "—will be unforgettable."

Her expression relaxed somewhat, and desire replaced the concern in her eyes. "I'm going to hold you to that."

He released her hands, unfastened his fly and snaked out of his slacks. After working his way onto the bed, he laced his hands together behind his head and told her, "Undress for me."

She slipped off the heels, shimmied out of her panties but when she reached for the stockings, he said, "Leave those on."

Fiona acknowledged the request with a sensuous smile. "Wow. This is a rush, stripping for a man. Anything else you want me to do?"

He held out his hand to her. "Come to me. Come with me."

She complied, straddling his thighs, leaving her completely open to his eyes, to his touch as he sifted through the shading between her legs, touching her again and again while watching her eyes grow hazy and soft, her full lips slack. But before the climax claimed her, Darin reached for the condom he'd left on the nightstand and sheathed himself.

"Now," he murmured, lifting her hips so he could guide her onto his shaft. He met some resistance and touched her again, more insistent this time, until her body gave in to the climax, pulling him into her heat.

Darin gritted his teeth in an effort to hold on to his sanity when she matched the movement of his hips as he sought his own release. She ground against him, her hair a wild tangle of curls surrounding her face as she took him on a journey into the deepest realm of pleasure. Pure, unrestrained pleasure unmatched by any lover he had ever known, and he had known many. Perhaps the feelings arose from wanting her more than he had wanted anything in a long while, from waiting for what seemed like infinity to have her. Perhaps because she made him feel truly alive for the first time in years.

In the past this was the point when he closed his eyes and immersed himself in the sensations, escaping to a place that included only physical release. Yet he kept his eyes open, drawn to the freedom he witnessed in Fiona's expression. That sense of liberation overtook him as his own climax began to build, harder and harder, faster and faster until everything around him disappeared, dissolved by this woman who had shed her inhibitions to give him what he needed, what he so desperately desired from her. Only her.

He pulled her down to join their lips as securely as they had joined their bodies. His heart thundered against his chest, his body shook when the climax ripped through him with the strength of a tempest. Fiona collapsed against him, and he clung to her as if she were a lifeline, his life force.

As the effects began to subside and reality took hold, Darin recognized he had been here before, replete, physically satisfied. Yet for the past few years, he had gone there alone, detached, a self-imposed seclusion that involved only primal need as protection against emotional involvement.

But as Fiona rested her cheek against his chest and he stroked her hair, as he drew in her perfume and felt the beat of her own heart against his, he realized he hadn't been alone at all. Tonight he had taken her with him.

Instinct told him to withdraw from her body, from her. Yet he could not consider pushing her away, not with her so sweet and soft in his arms. Only a few more moments, he told himself. Then he would leave her to return to the mission and the only life he had dared to embrace. A life that included no one.

Several minutes passed and he still made no move to leave. Her breathy sigh acted on him like a magical spell, beckoning him to remain until morning, to make love to her again. And again.

After a time she rolled onto her side, keeping her arm draped over his abdomen, her head tucked beneath his chin. All he had to do now was kiss her briefly and move from the bed, from her warmth. Still, he stayed.

"That was incredible," she murmured. "Definitely unforgettable."

Darin heartily agreed. Almost too incredible. "What time is it?" he asked.

Fiona lifted her head and peered at the bedside clock. "A little after eleven."

"I should go back to the casino," he said, surprised by the lack of enthusiasm in his tone.

Fiona feathered his neck with kisses. "You should stay here for a while, see what else comes up." She topped off the comment with a sultry stroke across his abdomen, traveling lower with each caress.

Darin laid his palm on her hand to stop her downward progress, otherwise he would again disregard his duty. "I should continue the search. Birkenfeld could return here at midnight."

Rising up onto one elbow, she stared down at him, disappointment in her eyes. "And that's still an hour away." She winked. "We could find something interesting to do until then."

"I need more time to recover."

She sent a direct look at his growing erection. "Well, you could have fooled me."

Darin rolled to his side and cupped her jaw in his palm. "Were you not completely satisfied?"

"Oh, yeah, but you've turned me into this wild creature who just can't seem to get enough of you."

"Then you wish more from me?"

"I'll take whatever you're willing to give."

He outlined her lips with a fingertip then did the same to her nipples. "Perhaps we can continue this later, after I've made sure the fugitive has not returned."

She pretended to pout. "You know, I like this guy less and less. But I do owe him one big favor."

Darin frowned. "What would that be?"

"If it wasn't for him, I wouldn't have met you. And frankly I wouldn't have wanted to miss that for the world."

Nor would Darin, but her serious tone made him uncomfortable. "Someday you will find a man who will treat you with respect and love."

"You've treated me with respect, and I appreciate that more than you know."

His frame went rigid as the emotional wall began to materialize. "Respect is all that I can give you, Fiona."

She sat up and pushed her hair out of her face. "Have I asked you for anything more, Darin?"

Hearing her say his given name only served to threaten his resistance. Many women had called him that before, yet it had not sounded so right. "No, you have not asked me for more." But he saw something in her eyes akin to love, or perhaps he was only imagining its presence. Still, he had to get away before he acknowledged that what he felt for her was developing into something he did not welcome. Something he could not afford to accept.

He worked his way to the edge of the bed and retrieved his

slacks from the floor, then stood. Without turning around, he said, "I will dress and go back downstairs. If I do not act now, I fear he could slip away again."

"You're afraid of more than that."

He spun around. "I am afraid of nothing."

She pulled the sheet up, concealing her body. "Maybe you're not afraid of deviants and criminals. But you are afraid to love."

How well she knew him. How well she could see through the guise he had so effectively used as a shield. "I have neither the time nor the desire for that emotion."

Wrapping the sheet around her, she left the bed and stood before him. "You're afraid of it, simple as that. You're scared to death of it. Why is that, Darin?"

He wasn't certain how to respond, so he said nothing at all.

She framed his jaw in her palm. "Did someone hurt you at one time? Maybe the woman named Tamra?"

"No."

"But you did love her."

"Yes," he replied, shocked by the ease of the admission.

"She broke your heart. Is that it?"

She had done nothing but love him as completely as any woman could love a man. And he had loved her the same. "She is a part of my past that I do not care to resurrect."

"Then she did leave you."

"Yes, but not in the way that you imagine."

"I can't imagine her leaving you at all considering you obviously loved her a great deal. I can see it in your eyes. Some women would die for that kind of commitment."

And Tamra had died because of her commitment to him. "She left because she had no choice."

"Everyone has choices, Scorpio."

"Her choice was taken away from her. And so was her life."

With that he gathered his discarded tuxedo and strode into the bathroom before he revealed everything to Fiona, including his failure to protect the woman who had captured his heart and won his love. Before Fiona knew that, in a few desperate moments, while he'd watched, that same woman had been torn from his life.

He refused to feel anything beyond fondness for Fiona, for if he did, he could very well face his greatest fear—losing someone else that he loved once she realized how flawed he had been, and still was.

Yet in the deepest recesses of his soul, in a place where he harbored memories of the past and the power of love, he wondered if perhaps he was already too late.

Nine

Fiona had never seen pain that intense in a man's eyes. Had never heard such abject grief even though he had tried to mask it with an even tone. She had been right. Darin was afraid to love, and with good reason. Death, not careless disregard, had taken the woman he loved from him.

That did nothing to assuage Fiona's wish that he was capable of loving her back. No matter how hard she'd fought it, she was starting to fall in love with him.

Starting? She'd already taken that leap as easily as if she'd been pole vaulting over a crack in the sidewalk.

While she perched on the edge of the bed wearing nothing but the sheet, the bathroom door opened and Scorpio came out dressed in the tuxedo, sans tie. Even though he wasn't smiling and didn't seem remotely pleased despite their incredible lovemaking, he still looked no less gorgeous.

"Going somewhere?" Fiona asked, affecting a casualness she didn't feel.

Without affording her even a cursory glance, he walked to

the dresser mirror and repositioned the square of linen on his head and secured it with the ornate gold band. "I told you, I will be leaving now to return to the casino. After my departure, you should lock the door and not answer it unless you are certain it is me." His tone was devoid of emotion, dispassionate. Heartbreaking.

She gripped the sheet tightly in her fists. "I'm going with you."

"No, you are not." He turned and gave her a hard look. "From this point forward, I will work alone."

Anger seeped in, splintering Fiona's former euphoria. "That's the way you like it, isn't it, Darin? Always alone. Always running away, this time from me."

He folded his arms across his broad chest and stared at her as if she were a petulant child. "I have been charged with apprehending a criminal. You've known that from the beginning. When I have accomplished that, I will be gone."

She swallowed around the lump in her throat. "Yeah. Here today, gone tomorrow, chasing after the next villain, but still running."

He slipped his wallet and keys into his pocket. "I will call to check on you."

She bolted to her feet. "Don't bother. I wouldn't want you to put yourself out on my account."

"It is my duty to keep you safe."

"I don't think it was duty that put us in bed together."

"I do not remember you protesting our recent activities."

"Activities?" For the first time in her life, she knew what it meant to see red beyond the color of her hair. "You mean lovemaking, don't you? Oh, wait. You wouldn't mean lovemaking because you're terrified of love. And I pity you for that."

His eyes looked like a firestorm. "I do not need your pity."

"And you don't need me, either, right?"

"My life does not accommodate need or love of another person."

She took a few steps forward until she was standing directly in front of him and breezed a fingertip over his clenched jaw. "I dare you, Scorpio."

His hands open and closed into tight fists at his sides, as if he was struggling not to reach for her. "Dare me to do what?"

"I dare you not to touch me." She slid a fingertip from the top button on his shirt down his belly then over the ridge beneath his slacks. "And I double dare you not to fall in love with me."

He clasped her hand and held it over his heart, which thrummed against his chest. "I find dares unappealing."

She untucked the sheet with her free hand and let it fall to the floor, leaving her completely naked. "But you don't find me unappealing, do you?"

Indecision warred in his dark, dark eyes as his gaze roamed over her body, then came back to her face. "True, I find you very appealing. That should be obvious by now. But again, I have no use for love."

Releasing his grip on her hand, he limped away without saying another word. But the slam of the hotel door told Fiona she had gotten to him on some level. And she would be damned if she sat alone in an empty hotel room without him.

Fiona quickly dressed in the evening gown and the stiletto heels invented by some sick dominatrix or a sadistic man. Minor payment for being in Scorpio's presence, whether he admitted he wanted her with him or not. Maybe he couldn't love her, but she did love him enough to make sure he was okay.

After slipping the spare room key into her purse and sliding the strap over her shoulder, she strode out of the hotel room, bound for a mission that didn't involve maniacs. Bound and determined to find Scorpio and force him to see the logic in her joining him. If he wanted her back in the room, then he would have to carry her there. And after that, she would pull out all the stops, use her feminine wiles and convince him that his time would be better spent in bed instead of chasing after a madman who was probably long gone.

She walked with head held high, with confidence and control—until she got to the elevator. She glanced at the doorway leading to the stairs, then back at the doors leading to the chamber of horrors. If she wanted to get to Scorpio quickly, she would have to convene her courage and banish her phobia for the ride down to the lobby.

Fiona willed her breathing to steady, told herself that she now had some mighty fine memories of what could be accomplished in an elevator to see her to the first floor. After all, what was the worst thing that could happen? Oh, she might hyperventilate a moment. She could start biting her nails again. She could go into a regular screaming-bloody-murder fit.

Nothing would happen other than when the elevator arrived, she was going to grow up and get on the thing.

After another deep breath, she pressed the down button, prepared to enter the vehicle that would take her to the man she wanted more than life itself—even if he didn't want her.

A sense of foreboding as sharp as a machete impaled Darin as he left the elevator on the ground floor. He wrote it off as an illogical need to be with Fiona, as if he could not survive without her by his side. Ridiculous. Insane. He worked alone. He did not need her company, even if he admittedly craved it. Right now he must search the premises for Birkenfeld. Wait in the shadows and hope for his appearance.

As he walked the corridor leading to the casino, his ankle throbbed with the effort. But with every step he took toward his goal, his instincts shouted danger, blocking the pain from his mind.

Well-honed instincts turned him around, sent him back toward the elevator to see about Fiona, to make certain she was safe. Then he would return. Then he would resume the search. If all else failed, including his resistance to Fiona's charms, he would begin again tomorrow.

As he reached the bank of elevators, he punched the button twice, impatient for the car to heed his call. He stepped back and noted that only two of the four seemed to be operating at present. Considering that most of the die-hard gamblers were sequestered in the casino and not traveling to the top-floor restaurant, he assumed this was common practice.

The seconds ticked off slowly and with each passing moment, Darin's concern escalated. His intuition had never before failed him, the reason why he trusted it now. Something was wrong. Terribly wrong.

Backing away a few more steps, he looked up as one car began its descent from the upper floors—and immediately spotted someone standing at the glass wall, looking out over the lobby, palms flattened against the surface as if trying to escape. After it traveled a few more floors, he identified the party as a woman. But not just any woman.

Fiona.

Perhaps that was what his instincts had been telling him, that her stubbornness had driven her onto the elevator alone so she could seek him out. Although he should be furious over her refusal to follow his directives, he was pleased to know she was safe. Until someone came up behind her.

Again Darin experienced a great deal of relief when he noted the figure was another woman. As best he could tell, a matriarchal type who wore sensible shoes and loose-fitting clothing. Nonthreatening and probably kindly, considering she was conversing with Fiona as they neared the lower level.

Then Darin saw the presumed "woman" grab Fiona and hold the blade at her throat. Saw the demonic eyes and the vicious, sardonic smile as she ripped the wig away and tossed it aside.

Birkenfeld's eyes. Birkenfeld's smile. Birkenfeld dressed as a woman.

And Fiona, who had fulfilled Darin's fantasies and captured a good deal of his reluctant heart, looked panic-stricken, while Darin could do nothing but stare.

When the elevator halted on the second floor and the pair disappeared from sight, fury and fear and determination propelled him forward. He sprinted toward the stairwell in hopes of intercepting before the deviant could harm Fiona, praying for the first time in years that he would not be too late.

He slammed back the door and took the stairs two at a time, stumbling on the landing and clawing at the wall to keep his balance. He cursed his injured ankle, cursed Birkenfeld for taking another innocent female victim when his battle should be with him.

The man was a coward. An insane, spineless, pathetic example of a man. And he would pay dearly.

Darin drew his gun and threw open the door simultaneously, finding the hallway that housed conference rooms empty. He suspected Birkenfeld would take Fiona into one of those chambers and await Darin's arrival. Or perhaps he would have Darin believe that and escort her somewhere else.

The sound of the familiar voice shouting, ''I have to get out of here!'' spun Darin toward the opposite end of the hallway where he spotted a service elevator, the doors in the process of closing, but not before he once again saw Birkenfeld holding Fiona captive, the blade still at her throat.

And Sheikh Darin Shakir came face-to-face with his greatest fear once more.

Fiona's lungs burned as she struggled for air, the walls closing in on her as the knife bit into her neck, her mind caught in a web of confusion. Everything had happened so fast. She'd entered the main elevator, proud that she had found the courage and somewhat relieved to discover she wouldn't be alone on her journey.

After a friendly hello to her female companion, she'd turned toward the glass and commented on the impressive statue of the man panning for gold in the fountain that served as the focal point in the lobby.

Fiona hadn't given the silence a second thought; after all, the woman hadn't seemed too affable in the boutique. She hadn't worried that her conversation had been one-sided; that hadn't ceased her nervous chatter. She had even begun to relax when she'd caught sight of Scorpio standing in the lobby, looking up at her with his midnight eyes and an expression that showed he'd been happy to see her, much to her surprise and delight. But the sense of satisfaction had faded away when the arms had come around her. Hairy arms threaded with thick veins. Brutal arms that had held her so forcefully she thought she might faint from the pressure on her lungs and ribs.

Only then had she looked back and registered the woman wasn't a woman at all—she was a man with features that might have been deemed handsome except for the satanic eyes glaring at her from the owl-like glasses.

"So we meet again," he'd said, his voice equally evil as he'd discarded the glasses and wig.

Fiona hadn't spoken another word, even when he'd yanked her off the main elevator and shoved her into the one where they now stood. Only then had she voiced her fear, yelled at him to let her out, let her go. And he had only laughed.

He wasn't laughing now but he was mumbling, "Stupid Shakir. I've got you now. Come and get me. Come and get your whore."

Fiona realized that Shakir must be Scorpio's real name. Darin Shakir most likely. And no doubt she was the designated whore. This maniac could think what he would about her now, but he might change his mind later because as soon as she had the opportunity, she would fight him. As soon as they arrived wherever they were going, she would land a proper punch in an improper place, gouge his eyes if she had to, do something to survive. Anything to live until Scorpio showed up. If he showed up.

He would. He had to. But if he didn't, then she would have to make it on her own. And if she did end up dead, her biggest regret would be waiting so long to tell him how she felt about him. Now she might never have the chance.

The doors opened to what appeared to be a dimly lit, deserted basement storage area lined with shelves that contained various cleaning supplies and equipment. Birkenfeld muttered, "Walk, whore," then shoved Fiona forward. She stumbled but caught herself before she landed face first on the cement floor, thinking this might be her chance at escape, until she felt the knife at her back.

"Keep moving," he said. "Don't turn around or I'll kill you."

"You are really something, Dr. B," she said, her tone dripping with sarcasm to mask her fear. "That's really clever, a disgusting doctor in drag. But I have to say, you don't make a very good-looking woman."

"Shut up!"

Although she recognized she should stop taunting him, she didn't want to. If he was going to kill her, she might as well get in a few digs. "I bet you look like your mother. Did your mother steal babies, too? Was she a blackjack junkie?"

He poked the tip of the knife in her lower back, not quite breaking the skin but coming close. "Stop talking!" His voice had an edge of hysteria. "Stop laughing!"

Odd, Fiona hadn't laughed at all but obviously he thought she was laughing at him. The man was certifiable, ready for the loony bin, and decidedly dangerous. She considered that as they continued on, heading who knew where. Probably a hell of his own making.

If he tried to force her into a vehicle, Fiona decided then and there she would refuse to go because that would mean certain doom. Even if he did manage to stab her, she would stand a better chance at being rescued in the open. If he intended to go someplace out in the open, and that wasn't very likely.

The thought of him locking her up somewhere confining, like a closet, almost brought Fiona to her knees. She pushed that fear from her mind. Considering his continued nonsensical tirade about the evils of women—"All whores" he said repeatedly—she had much more to be afraid of at the moment, namely that he would completely lose it and attempt to cut her to shreds before they took another step.

She needed to stall for time and searched her addled brain, trying to remember his first name. Roman. That was it. "You know, Roman, these shoes are hurting my feet. You could stop a minute so I can take them off. We could go much faster then.''

He pushed the knife harder into her back and for a moment Fiona thought it was all over. ''Keep moving. Keep moving now. Go forward. Don't turn around or I'll kill you here, before Shakir can watch.''

Bile rose in Fiona's throat when she realized Birkenfeld's sick plan—to set a trap for Scorpio and kill her before his eyes. Oh, God. She couldn't let that happen. As much as she wanted him to come to her rescue, she didn't want him to witness her death. But how could she possibly prevent that? She knew Darin Shakir well enough to know he wouldn't leave her alone. He would find her, whatever it took.

''Okay, Roman, I'll keep moving. You don't have to keep sticking me, though.''

''I'll kill you soon.'' His voice was surprisingly calm, eerily so, and that sent chills snaking up Fiona's spine.

''Mind telling me where we're going?'' she asked, hating the tremble in her voice.

He laughed. A skin-crawling, maniacal laugh. ''Someplace dark.''

When Darin reached the bowels of the building, he tried to push through a heavy door but found it locked. Overcome with frustration, he pounded his fist into the metal, breaking the skin at his knuckles. He was numb to the pain in both his hand and ankle. He felt nothing but desperation and the bitter taste of impending disaster.

He kicked the door once, twice, yet it failed to budge. Frantically he searched the area, coming upon a transparent case containing a fire extinguisher and an ax, provided to break the glass, mounted on the wall. After shoving his gun into the holster, he grabbed the ax and broke through the small rectangular window in the door. He reached inside, groping for the release that continued to evade him for a time until finally, he hit the metal bar and shoved the door open.

He sprinted through the empty corridor, disregarding his aching foot pounding the concrete as he tuned his senses in to the surroundings, listening for voices yet hearing nothing. He picked up his pace, running as fast as his injuries would allow, stumbling twice, then halting when he heard a closing door in the distance. He advanced toward the sound, hoping he was heading closer to Fiona and Birkenfeld and not away from them. Once he reached the exit leading outside, he paused to listen once more and discerned muffled voices, one male, one female.

He had found them.

Yet he faced a certain dilemma if he walked out the door. Birkenfeld could be armed with a gun. He could slash Fiona's throat before Darin had a chance to fire his own gun. He would not risk it. He could not watch her die, helpless once more to prevent it. He would find a way to save her.

Stepping back, he looked around and saw two elongated windows set into the wall several feet above his head, almost to the top of the high ceiling. If he could reach one and open it, he could fire off a shot and hit his mark.

He had been trained by the best during his military career. He had learned to shoot accurately, with deadly force, showing no mercy, his goal after his attempts to rescue Tamra from Habib had failed.

Tonight he would not fail. He *could* not fail.

Propelled by his own demons, Darin tore off his jacket, yanked off his shoes, then retrieved a nearby ladder and propped it against the wall. He climbed to the top rung and grasped the thick brick ledge surrounding the window above his head, hoisting himself up. He perched on his knees leaving barely enough room to maneuver.

Slowly, quietly, he unlatched the locks and slid the window open, blessedly with ease. He peered into the night to find a delivery bay down below as well as Birkenfeld who had Fiona pushed up against the trailer of an eighteen-wheel truck, his back to the building.

The bastard. Darin could only imagine how Fiona was feel-

ing at that moment, trapped and alone. If only he could let
her know he was there, that she wasn't alone. But he could
not without further risking her life.

Darin removed the Beretta, pulled back the slide and took
aim. Sweat rolled down his forehead and gathered on his
palms where he maintained a two-handed grip on the gun. He
disregarded the burning in the pit of his stomach. But he could
not disregard the limited light or the fact that although he
could kill Birkenfeld with a single shot in the back, the bullet
could penetrate and hit Fiona, as well.

He waited for an opportunity, waited for what seemed an
interminable amount of time while his mind cataloged his
options. He needed to distract Birkenfeld and hoped that he
moved away from Fiona. He would have to be quick, have to
be sure. He had no room for mistakes. If he missed, Birkenfeld could turn on Fiona with the knife, and once again Darin
would be faced with the same situation as before.

He reached into his pants pocket for his keys to toss out
the window in hopes of diverting Birkenfeld's attention from
Fiona. But first he came upon the round stone Fiona had given
him for luck, which would provide a better distraction. And
if that luck prevailed, Fiona might be afforded an opportunity
to move away so that he could take a shot.

Darin rolled the stone in his left palm as if that might provide good fortune and end the curse that had befallen the men
in his family. Normally he would not have believed in something so imprudent, but then, he had never believed his life
would have taken such a drastic turn eight years before. He
would not have believed he would find himself in this familiar
predicament again, after he had sworn not to.

Yet here he was, charged with protecting a woman whom
he cared a great deal for, and he had limited time to achieve
that goal now that Birkenfeld seemed to be growing more
agitated, evidenced by his ranting.

Darin threw the stone side-handed as hard as he could, with
as much accuracy as he could, considering the limited light.

Amazingly it hit the intended target, the truck's rear bumper, and bounced away.

Birkenfeld's head snapped toward the sound, yet he did not move as Darin had hoped. Suddenly the criminal doubled over, then stumbled to one side, clutching for the truck to regain his balance and in the process, dropping the knife. In a split second that seemed like eternity, Darin took his best shot, aiming for Birkenfeld, who straightened and turned with lightning speed to lunge for Fiona.

The bullet hit Birkenfeld's neck, sending the criminal forward with the force of the impact. When he landed at Fiona's feet, Fiona screamed, a tortured, keening cry. She backed up, sank to the ground then cried Darin's name. His real name.

Darin needed to get to her. Needed to comfort her, let her know everything would be all right. He shoved the gun back into the holster, climbed down the ladder and rushed out the door, only to be met by a host of security personnel immediately outside the building.

One massive guard grabbed Darin and wrenched his arm behind his back as if he were the criminal, sending a pain shooting through his shoulder to add to the one in his foot and fist. When he struggled against his confinement, the guard punched him in the stomach, almost crippling him.

"He's the good guy," Fiona cried out and rushed forward, only to be held back by another uniformed guard.

When Darin reached for her extended hand, their fingertips touched before the guard pulled Darin's other arm around to clamp handcuffs on his wrists. "Keep back, ma'am. We don't want him to hurt you."

"He didn't hurt me, you jerk," she said. "You've got the wrong man." She turned and pointed at Birkenfeld, crumpled on the ground, a man crouched beside him. "That's the criminal. Darin killed him before he could kill me."

Darin needed to hold her more than he needed the air he could not seem to draw into his lungs because of the blow to his belly. Because of the restraints, he could only stand helplessly by and watch her struggling with her misery.

The guard grabbed Darin by the shoulders and shoved him against the wall. "What's your name?"

When he could finally recover his voice and respiration, he said, "I am Darin Shakir, and what she says is true. I have been working with the FBI to apprehend this—" he sucked in another ragged breath "—this criminal. His name is Roman Birkenfeld and he's wanted on numerous federal charges."

He pulled the Beretta from Darin's holster and held it up. "So who the hell are you with?"

"An organization in Texas. If you will release my hands, I will contact a Bureau agent who will verify my identity."

He handed the gun off to the guard who was struggling to keep Fiona at bay. "I ain't releasing you until I know for sure you're legit."

"Are you injured, Fiona?" Darin managed through the fog of exhaustion clouding his brain. "Did he hurt you?"

"No. I'm fine."

The man who had checked Birkenfeld approached, shining a flashlight in Darin's eyes. "The guy's dead. According to dispatch, Vegas PD is coming around the building now."

"Get that light out of his eyes!" Fiona shouted, still firmly in the grasp of a guard. "Can't you see that he's hurt?"

"We will be all right," Darin told Fiona as she sent him a forlorn look. "This will all be reconciled soon. Are you certain you are not hurt?"

"I'm okay," she replied, her voice laced with tears.

To Darin she did not sound okay but at least she was alive. Still, it would take time for her to recover, and he would do everything in his power to help her tonight, before he returned to Texas tomorrow. Guilt plagued him over the prospect of leaving her alone to deal with the events of the past few days—guilt and another emotion he was only beginning to recognize and understand.

Fiona was strong, and she would survive without him. Yet the thought of leaving her prompted an ache in his soul that was ten times worse than the pain of his injuries.

A swirl of multicolored lights and the sounds of approach-

ing sirens served to enhance his frustration. He did not need
this turmoil. He had only done his job, ending Birkenfeld's
reign of terror. He did need help. He needed to call Kent. But
most of all, he needed to hold Fiona. To recapture his own
strength through her.

And he would, as soon as his hands were free.

Fiona thought they were never going to let Scorpio go.
After she answered their questions, she leaned against the
hood of the police cruiser while they interrogated Darin inside
the vehicle. In a haze Fiona watched the coroner's car carry
Birkenfeld away, a surreal scene when she considered the
front of her new dress was covered in his blood. She chose
not to think about it, otherwise she would fall apart.

Fiona felt wasted, sapped of energy and terrified by what
she had witnessed and what had almost happened. If Scorpio
hadn't shown up when he had, she would probably be the one
they were carting away in a body bag.

Hugging her arms tightly around her middle did not alleviate the uncontrollable shakes. The men who had been so
concerned earlier seemed to have forgotten about her after the
paramedics had checked her out and pronounced her physically okay. She couldn't exactly say the same for her current
mental state.

Right now she wanted to go back to the room and wash
away the reminders of this horrible night and the horrible man
who had held her captive. A dead man, thanks to Scorpio.
Maybe she should start thinking of him by his proper name,
Darin Shakir. Regardless, after this was all over, she would
always remember him as Scorpio, her brave, seductive
stranger. Her hero.

Finally Scorpio surfaced from the car, and a police officer
removed his handcuffs. A tall, lanky man wearing a suit approached the vehicle and stood beside him, speaking in low
tones. Fiona pushed away from the hood and moved closer to
hear what he was saying.

"My apologies for the interrogation, Sheikh Shakir."

Sheikh Shakir? Fiona's mouth dropped open. No way. No how. Oh, wow.

"I understand your caution," Scorpio said. "I hope that Alexander Kent has cleared everything up."

"He has and had I been notified immediately, we would have avoided this. We appreciate your organization's assistance in apprehending Birkenfeld. I'm sorry that you were forced to shoot him, at least in front of an innocent woman."

Scorpio turned and sent Fiona a meaningful look. "Actually, she was instrumental in his capture. She somehow managed to disable him."

Fiona inched a little closer to his side. "It's known as a high-heel-applied-to-the-instep-and-a-knee-to-the-crotch maneuver. Works every time."

The stranger smiled. "I'm Agent Mills with the Bureau. Thank you for your assistance, Ms.?"

Fiona took his extended hand for a brief shake. "Powers."

"Did you sustain any injuries, Ms. Powers?"

"Only to my sense of security."

Scorpio wrapped an arm around her shoulder. "You are safe now. He can no longer hurt you."

But Scorpio could, Fiona decided, by leaving her behind tomorrow. In the meantime she needed some comfort. She needed to forget. And she wanted to do that in Darin Shakir's capable arms. *Sheikh* Darin Shakir. That was going to take a while to get used to, but she didn't have more than a few hours left in his company. She intended to make the best of every blasted minute, and she would try to make enough memories to last a lifetime. Good memories to overcome the bad.

"Can we go back to the room now?" she asked.

Darin regarded Mills. "Are we free to go?"

The agent gestured toward the hotel. "Sure. I'll let you know if we need anything else, but after talking to Kent, I think we have all our questions answered."

"Good." Darin released Fiona, stepped forward and shook the agent's hand. "Thank you for your assistance."

"No problem. Only, next time I hope you'll consider working closer with us in order to avoid this kind of situation."

"There will not be a next time. After I return to Texas to report in, I will be traveling to Europe and staying there indefinitely."

Fiona's heart fell to her feet. Not only was he leaving Vegas, he was leaving the country. Leaving her behind without a second thought.

Yet as they walked back into the hotel, arms around each other's waists, he acted as though he didn't intend to let her go, at least not now. That lifted Fiona's spirits somewhat, although she was having trouble battling persistent tears from the horrors she'd recently experienced and the knowledge that she would soon say goodbye to him for good.

After they reached the lobby elevators, Darin turned to her and rested his palms on her shoulders. "Do you wish to take the stairs?"

She glanced at his sock-covered feet. "Considering you're still gimpy and barefoot, that's not a great idea. By the way, where are your shoes and jacket?"

"In the basement. I took them off to climb into the window."

She met his gaze, so dark yet almost soft. "That was quick thinking, but you're going to lose your deposit on the tux unless you go back for them."

"I will pay for the suit."

"I guess that won't be a problem since you happen to be a sheikh, which explains why you looked so natural playing one. Why didn't you tell me sooner?"

"Because that, too, is a part of my past. Other than the more-than-adequate funds my legacy has afforded me, I have no use for nobility."

"Define 'more-than-adequate funds.'"

"Enough to purchase this hotel. And most of the hotels on the Strip. Combined."

And Fiona had been worried about the money she'd pilfered for the dress. She still intended to pay him back before he left. "Well, my, my, he's not only sexy and a prince, he's also filthy rich."

He pulled her fast against him. "He is also very much in need of your company."

"I can live with that." She wasn't sure how she was going to live without him. She would, only because she had to.

Easy come, easy go. But nothing about saying goodbye to Darin Shakir would be easy. Right now she didn't want to think about that or consider anything but getting him alone. She wanted to make love with him once more, to forget that tonight she had seen a man die. That she had almost been killed by that same man had it not been for her rescuer.

Stepping out of his arms, Fiona reached down to remove the sadistic shoes and to conceal the tears trying to make a grandstand appearance.

"Do you not think it would be best to undress in our room instead of in the lobby?" he asked, a lightness in his voice that seemed almost strained.

She straightened and gave him a shaky smile. "This is only the preliminaries."

"Then I suggest we hurry." His smile turned seductive. "If we are lucky, we will be the only occupants in the elevator."

Fiona tossed her shoes over her shoulder, landing them in the fountain with a loud splash. "I think that's a great reason to hurry. And an even better reason to take the elevator."

He sent her a questioning look. "Then you are no longer afraid."

She draped her arms around his neck and kissed the dimple at the corner of his incredible mouth. "I've been trapped with a maniac, wielding a really big knife. I've watched that same maniac get shot and die. A little old elevator doesn't scare me anymore."

But the intensity of Fiona's feelings for Darin Shakir frightened her. And she would express them, if not with words, then with actions.

Ten

Fiona wasn't sure who was leaning more on whom as they walked the corridor to the suite. They'd ridden up the elevator in silence, in an embrace, content only to hold on tightly to each other. When they entered the hotel room, Scorpio continued to hold her for a time as if he didn't have the strength to do anything else. And that was okay with Fiona. As much as she wanted to make love with him, to lose herself in his touch, she would welcome this intimacy all night long. In his arms she felt safe and secure.

After a few minutes he finally eased his grasp but kept his arms around her. "I'll be leaving tomorrow," he said.

Hearing the words cemented the reality in Fiona's heart, and that made her hurt all over. "I know."

"If you would prefer I sleep somewhere else—"

"No. I want this last night with you."

He held her face in his palms and rubbed his thumbs along her jaw, the familiar gesture tearing at Fiona's heart. "Are you certain?" he asked.

"Yes. I'd like a few good memories to carry with me after the bad ones tonight."

His expression filled with remorse. "I am sorry I involved you in this. But I'm thankful that you are now safe."

"So am I. I'm also thankful I met you." Fiona tried to smile, yet it felt unnatural considering he would soon be gone from her life. "That was quite an adventure, huh?"

"More adventure than you or I bargained for."

She toyed with the top button of his shirt. "I wouldn't exactly refuse a certain kind of excitement that doesn't involve crazy criminals in drag and guns."

He breezed a kiss over her lips. "Neither would I."

"Then why are we standing here?"

Without another word, Scorpio took her by the hand and led her into the bedroom. Once there, he seated her on the edge of the mattress, his gaze raking over her, homing in on the bodice of the dress. His expression went stone cold.

Fiona looked down and noticed the dark blotches splattered over her cleavage. Birkenfeld's blood. She'd almost forgotten she still carried the reminders.

She looked up at Scorpio and saw something akin to torment in his eyes, as if he were reliving the moments, both those tonight and those years before. "It's okay. I'll clean it up."

When she started to stand, he stopped her by nudging her gently back onto the edge of the bed. "I will do it."

"I'm okay. Really."

"I would prefer to do it."

She lifted her shoulder in a nonchalant shrug when all the while she was battling tears over his kindness, his care. "Okay."

After retiring to the bathroom for a few minutes, Scorpio returned with a washcloth and knelt in front of her. With his free hand, he loosened the clasp at her neck and the bodice fell to her waist. Then he began bathing her, carefully, until all the remnants of the blood were gone. But instead of stand-

ing, Scorpio tossed the rag onto the table and regarded her
with intense dark eyes.

"Do you trust me, Fiona?"

"Yes."

"Then lie back on the bed."

Fiona did as he asked without hesitation because she did
trust him. With all her hammering heart, she did.

While she watched, he shed his shirt then slipped out of
his socks and slacks, leaving him completely nude before her.
Naked and aroused and beautiful. She took every detail to
memory, the breadth of his chest, the definition of his abdomen, the shading of masculine hair surrounding his sex. The
faint welt at his side and the bandage on his thigh served as
reminders of the night he had come into her life—a night that
had changed her in many ways.

He leaned over and removed her dress, then her panties,
hovering above her a few moments to take a long glance down
her trembling body. After he leaned over and kissed her lips,
long and leisurely, he propped two pillows beneath her shoulders and moved onto the bed at her feet.

"Do you trust me?" he asked again, stroking his fingertips
up and down her instep.

"Yes," Fiona managed on a ragged breath.

After bending her knees and nudging them apart with his
palms, he trailed his warm lips over the inside of her thighs,
first one, then the other, progressing upward over her pelvis
before bringing his mouth to rest below her navel. She drew
in a quick breath and released it on a gasp when he pressed
his lips against the shading at the apex of her legs.

He lifted his head and fixed his black eyes on her face.
"You have nothing to fear now," he murmured. "I will give
you no pain, only pleasure."

Fiona gripped the covers at her sides and prepared for that
pleasure, her eyes closed against the onslaught of sensation
as his mouth covered her intimately and his soft, skilled
tongue divined her flesh. All remembrance of tonight's horrors disappeared on a strong current of desire—and love for

this man who was taking her beyond all limits. A moan crawled up her throat and escaped as impending climax drove her to the edge of rationality, drove her to a place she had never really been before. Trembling turned to shaking, cold to heat, apprehension to elation under his mastery. And even though Fiona didn't want any of it to end, she couldn't hold back any more than she could hold on to her heart.

The climax consumed her, hard and furious, lifting her hips up from the force of it. But Scorpio didn't stop. Didn't even pause or let up long enough for her to catch her breath. He simply kept her captive with his mouth, with the ebb and flow of his tongue until once more, another climax claimed her as strong as the first.

Fiona covered her face with her palms to stop herself from crying out.

He pulled her hands from her face and held them against the solid wall of his chest. "Do you wish to continue?"

How could she not when he had shown her such total gratification? How would she ever find another man who moved her the way that he did, body and soul? Truthfully she probably never would.

"Yes," she murmured, touching his cheek. "I want all of you."

Darin kissed each of her palms. "And you will have all of me."

No, not all of him, Fiona thought. She would never have his heart. Beyond tonight, this was all they would have.

In silent mourning of the inevitable loss, in silent praise of his beauty, she watched him take the condom from the bedside table and tear into the package with fingers that appeared to be shaking, belying his calm exterior. He was so tough at times, yet Fiona had begun to see the fissures in his emotional armor, like now as he came back to the bed and took her in his arms, stroking her cheek and hair with such tenderness. She could look at his face forever, could lose herself in him for hours at a time, or at least for the few brief hours before dawn.

"I need you," she whispered as they faced each other.

Darin realized that Fiona had no idea how much he needed her. He shook with the force of his need, so much so he wanted to plunge inside her. But he silently cautioned himself to practice restraint, for as much as he needed to be inside her, he needed her complete trust more.

After moving over her, he braced on extended arms, keeping his lower body angled away. "Do you still trust me?" he asked again.

"Yes," she murmured.

He moved his legs on either side of her hips, waiting to hear any protest or to see any fear. Instead she gripped his shoulders and pulled him toward her, welcoming him with a tender smile and vibrant green eyes hazy with the desire he knew was reflected in his own eyes.

Darin entered her with a slow glide, then paused to look at Fiona, her hair a russet halo framing her face, contrasting with the white satin pillow. She did not look wary or uncomfortable, but he had to be certain before he continued. "Are you—"

"Don't hold back. Promise me?"

"I promise," he said, making a vow to a woman for the first time in eight years. If only he could give her more than this act, more of himself. All of himself.

Darin slid his hands beneath her bottom, bringing Fiona up to meet his thrusts. They moved together, uninhibited, their bodies joined, as well as their mouths, as if they could devour each other. As if they could not receive enough of this pleasure to be satisfied. As if they had always been lovers.

"More," Fiona murmured when Darin broke the kiss to draw a breath. "I want to feel you more."

Darin pulled her legs around his waist and set a wilder rhythm in answer to her plea. His heart thrashed in his chest as he journeyed closer and closer to climax. A mild oath directed at his body's impatience filtered through his brain, the final coherent thought as he slipped farther away, farther into a world created by Fiona's touch, her scent, her wet heat surrounding him, pulling him deeper into oblivion until he could no longer fight the searing release.

He shuddered over the impact, held her closer although he felt as if they were still not close enough. A long time had passed since he had been so attuned to a woman, so replete that he felt almost weak. Yet he still craved her nearness, even as his pulse slowed and his respiration returned in slow measure.

He continued to hold her close to his heart until he became mindful that she was taking all of his weight, remembering how much she despised feeling trapped. But when he shifted to move off her, she hung on to him and whispered, "Stay."

And he did, wishing that he could remain with her indefinitely. Until he could once more be the man that he had been before tragedy had stolen his faith and shattered his world. A man who had freely loved and been loved in return.

Tonight Fiona had given him her total trust. Tomorrow he would leave her to return to Texas before departing to Obersburg. He had no choice; he'd given the royal family his word. Aside from that, believing he could open himself enough to be the man she needed was nothing more than an elusive dream, even though what he felt for her had begun to seem surprisingly real. And for the first time in years, he felt alone no more.

"What time is it?"

Fiona posed the question with her cheek resting against Darin's shoulder, her fingers drawing random designs through the mat of hair on his chest. She was too boneless to lift her head, too afraid to look at the bedside clock and discover that the time for him to leave had come.

"Two hours before dawn," he said, brushing a kiss across her forehead.

Fiona wished she could turn back time, return to the distant past when they had enjoyed each other's company without the threat of a criminal hanging over them. Go back a few hours when they had showered together until the water had turned tepid, touching and exploring with greedy hands and mouths. They'd returned to bed and eaten cheesecake together, compliments of room service and on the house because of Darin's heroism, according to the waiter who'd delivered the tray.

Scorpio had laughed when Fiona fed him with their shared fork, and he moaned when she'd done some terribly wicked things with the burgundy sauce lining the dessert plate. And to think she hadn't cared all that much for raspberries, but she had cared about Darin Shakir enough to return the pleasure he had shown her. But he'd only allowed the intimacy for a few moments before they'd made love again, utilizing the pink condom provided by Peg, again bringing on their laughter.

Right now Fiona no longer felt like laughing. She seriously wanted to sob, to beg him to stay a little longer—forever. If only she could find the courage to tell him she loved him, but so far that courage had escaped her.

She could find out a little more about him, if he was willing to talk. "Did you know your former fiancée long before she was...uh—"

"Killed?" His tone was as rigid as his frame. "For several years. We were to be married in a matter of weeks before the incident."

"If you don't mind me asking, how did it happen?"

If his silence was any indication, he did mind, so Fiona decided to let it go, until he said, "Tamra was shot by the man who had killed my uncle, the king. He was an extremist who'd opposed my uncle's forward thinking, a coward who preyed on a woman, who meant nothing to him, in order to punish the royal family. That day she was meeting me in the village for dinner. We were celebrating the news she had received that morning. She was going to have my child."

Oh, God. "She was pregnant?"

"Yes, and she was so happy. I could see it in her face as she began running toward me. Then I saw the car and I knew it was him, but there was nothing I could do to prevent it since I was unarmed. I had also dismissed my bodyguards so that we could have the evening alone. When the sound of a single gunshot rang out, I could do nothing for her aside from holding her in my arms and watching her die.'' He ran a hand over his eyes, as if trying to erase the images or maybe even in an effort to stop the tears.

It was becoming all too clear to Fiona what Darin had suffered and why he had so effectively closed himself off to emotions and to his legacy.

She remained silent, determined not to put him through any more torture, but he chose to continue without any prodding. ''I trained with the military for a year, learned how to shoot well, then I joined a group of soldiers assigned to track him. He almost escaped when one man fired at him and missed. But I did not.''

''I guess that made you feel somewhat vindicated.''

''I felt nothing. No satisfaction. No joy in what I had done. Only a numbness that I have carried with me for some time now.''

That he still carried with him, Fiona decided. Obviously, she was not the woman to get him over his heartache, and that made her so very sad. She settled for kissing his lips and nestling close to his side, absorbing his heat and in some ways his grief. She had left behind a man and a mother who hadn't understood her, and now she had found a man who seemed to know and embrace all her secrets, yet he couldn't give anything to her beyond physical pleasure.

Just another chapter in the sad, sad story of Fiona's life.

''What time does your plane leave?'' Fiona asked as they walked hand in hand through the airport.

They traveled past a bank of slot machines creating a noisy furor that only added to Darin's sour mood. ''It should be here now,'' he said, slowing the pace.

Fiona looked around as they continued past several commercial gates. ''What airline?''

''It is a private plane.''

''I guess that shouldn't surprise me,'' she said.

They continued on in silence until they reached the area where Darin was directed to meet the plane. He spotted Alexander Kent immediately and beside him stood Ryan Evans, David Sorrenson, Clint Andover and Travis Whelan, all five of the Cattleman's Club members who had been involved in the mission with Darin from the beginning. He was taken aback by their appearance, since he'd expected only Alex to escort him back to Texas. Yet he shouldn't be shocked. Everything they had accomplished, they had done so as a team up until Darin had been assigned to track Birkenfeld.

Ryan held up a hand in a wave, but Darin stopped and faced Fiona. "My party has arrived."

Fiona glanced at the group and frowned. "Are all those guys law enforcement?"

"In a manner of speaking. We are all members of the same organization."

"A top secret organization, I take it."

"Yes."

Fiona sent him a bright smile that Darin took to memory. "And I suppose there's nothing I can do to make you talk?"

He leaned over and whispered, "You have already done that, and quite well."

"Anytime," she said, a hint of sadness in her tone. "I'll be here if you ever decide to come back to Vegas. If you ever need a friend."

Darin recognized that he did consider her a friend, as well as the consummate lover. He saw her as a woman he hated to leave more than she realized. A woman who had dissolved his defenses and touched a part of his soul. But he had to leave her. He had somewhere else to be, another mission in another country. Normally that would bring about anticipation. Today he lacked in enthusiasm.

"I have seen to it that your apartment will be repaired," he said.

"I can't go back there. I'm going to see if I can stay with Peg and Walt until I finish school in a few weeks."

"After you complete your studies, what will you do?" he asked.

"I hope to find a good job in a hotel. Maybe someday own my own place."

For some strange reason, Darin was hoping she would ask to come with him. "Then you will not be seeking adventure somewhere else?"

She released a humorless laugh. "I think I've had my fill of adventure for a while. I'll just be thankful for what I have. A nice dog, a decent job and a good future if I play my cards right."

He palmed her face and rubbed his thumb down her delicate jaw. "I wish you only the best of luck. I hope you have all that you seek in this lifetime."

She laid her palm on his hand and said, "And if there's ever anything I can do for you, just let me know."

"You can kiss me goodbye."

Once again she glanced at the men standing nearby, looking on with expectancy and blatant curiosity. "You mean you're going to put me in a lip lock right here in front of all the guys?"

Frankly, Darin did not care who witnessed their affection. He had no doubt he would bear the brunt of their questions on the trip back, but kissing Fiona one last time, holding her, would be well worth the harassment he would most surely endure from his friends.

On that thought, he kissed her deeply, releasing all the gratitude, all the desire, all the caring he felt for her in that moment.

Even when a whistle sounded along with, "We've got to go, Shakir," they kissed a few moments longer before parting, their gazes still fixed on each other. Darin longed for more time with her. He would like nothing better than to return to the hotel, spend the day in bed with her in his arms instead of the day on a plane with five men.

"Take care, Scorpio," Fiona said, then landed her palm on

his buttocks. "You have a really great derriere. See? I know some French, in case I ever get to Paris."

Darin brushed a kiss across her lips and gave her a smile. "I will miss you, Fiona. More than you know."

She stood on her toes and whispered in his ear, "And I love you, too, Darin Shakir."

With that Fiona turned and walked away, leaving Darin alone in stunned silence. She loved him, and he did not understand why she had waited so long to tell him. But worse, he felt the same about her, and he had not bothered to tell her. Yet somehow she had known, exactly as she had known his pain, his grief. She had dared him to love her, and he had effectively taken the bait.

A hand patted his back and Darin turned to find Ryan Evans standing beside him, the others gathering nearby. "Well, I'll be damned. Looks like the sheikh not only caught a criminal while he was here, he also caught a fine-looking redhead. Is that the woman Birkenfeld tried to kill?"

He craned his neck to watch Fiona until she disappeared from sight among the masses. "Yes, that is her. Fortunately, she was unharmed."

"Thanks to you," Kent said. "I'm assuming she's the one who aided you during the mission."

"Yes."

"What else did she aid you with, Shakir?" Sorrenson chimed in.

As suspected, the taunting had already begun, yet Darin was not in a tolerant mood. "She has been very accommodating."

"I just bet she has," Travis Whelan added, drawing the other men's laughter.

Darin's control shattered. "I will not abide any disrespect directed at Fiona Powers. She is a good woman and deserves to be treated as such."

Clint Andover, who'd been silent to this point, held up his hands, palms forward. "Darin, we're sorry. Obviously, you care a great deal for her."

"He's in love with her," Ryan added. "I see it all over that stony mug of his. I saw it when he looked at her. And if he knows what's good for him, he'll go after her before she gets away."

"Evans is right, Shakir," Travis said. "If you have feelings for her, and I'm guessing you do, don't throw it away. A good woman is a damn hard thing to find."

Their words whirled around in Darin's mind, even as he said, "I believe that all of you have found good women over the past few months. That could possibly disprove your theory."

"True, we have found good women," Kent said. "And that leaves you as the last man standing. So don't just stand here, go find her. Bring her back to Texas. Settle down with her. Have a couple of kids like your cousin, Ben, who by the way is a new father. Jamie had a boy last night."

Darin smiled when considering how proud Ben must be to have a son, although he could not imagine his cousin loving his latest child more than he loved his daughter. More than he loved his wife. Could Darin hope to have that bond with another woman? A family of his own? Would Fiona be amenable to joining him? And would he risk it all, his wanderlust and desire for justice, to go after her and find out if what she had said was true—that she loved him?

Yes. During this mission, justice had been served. And Darin no longer needed to atone for his failures—except for one. Leaving Fiona behind.

He turned and headed away from his friends, walking as quickly as his not-quite-healed ankle would allow.

"Where are you going, Shakir?" Ryan called after him.

Without turning around, he said, "I am going to see a woman about a future."

Fiona tipped her head against the steering wheel and let the tears, she had tried so hard to keep, free at last. They came in a rush, hot and bitter, biting into her cheeks as surely as the grief bit into her heart. Just as she composed herself enough to put the car in reverse and pull away, a sad song about saying goodbye came over the radio, and she cried some more.

Mars to Fiona.

She had to get a grip. Had to remember that when she'd met Darin Shakir, she'd known all along it would be a temporary thing. Had that stopped her from getting involved with him? Oh, no. She'd wanted a little adventure and she'd gotten it, knowing he was emotionally off-limits. Had that stopped her from falling in love with him? Of course not. Her stupid heart had led her right into that trap.

But it was too late for regrets. Besides, she would never regret meeting Darin Shakir, and she would never forget him. Not now. Not ever.

Pulling the rearview mirror toward her, she took a tissue and dabbed at the mascara smudged beneath her eyes. In a few hours she would see Lottie and Peg and get back to the business of finishing school while resuming her position in the bar. Then she would go on with her life, alone for the time being. Just the same-old, same-old, but only for a few weeks. Then the small-town girl with the big-time dreams would realize her goals and maybe even find someone who liked a little adventure, someone who was sexy and mysterious and not afraid to give himself to her.

Yeah, right. That was probably going to be as likely as Darin Shakir…

Walking out of the airport?

She closed her eyes and opened them slowly to peer into the mirror's reflection once more, believing that what she saw was simply a mirage or her imagination.

But he was real. Very, very real.

He emerged from the bright sunlight like some Arabian god bent on a mission to break the hearts of women around the world. He still wore all black, from his jacket to his cargo pants and boots. Aside from the slight limp, he walked with confidence, with purpose toward Fiona's car.

For a moment Fiona hoped that he was coming back for

her, but then she decided he'd probably forgotten something, although she couldn't imagine what. Had he discovered the missing money from his wallet? Damn, she knew she should've written him a check, but honestly, that had been the last thing on her mind, especially after their goodbye scene. All she'd wanted to do was run out of the terminal before she flung herself down onto the ground and cried a river right there in the waiting room. Right now all she wanted to do was fling herself at his feet.

He approached the car, and without hesitation tossed his bag to the ground, opened her door, then pulled her out and into his arms.

"Come with me," he said.

Surely she had moths in her ears. Or maybe it was the jet passing overhead. "What did you say?"

"Come with me back to Texas."

Texas? "Why?"

"To be with me."

Fiona fought the temptation to accept, to say yes without a second thought. But she had come too far to let her heart rule her head. "Look, Scorpio, that sounds like a really nice idea, but I have responsibilities here. To my school and my job. To myself. I can't just run off with you on a moment's notice."

"You told me you wanted adventure."

She couldn't deny that. She also couldn't deny that she wanted to be with him in the worst way. But she'd almost given up her dreams for one man; she couldn't do it for another. She'd seen her mother run off with several men, only to come back with her heart in pieces afterward. Then again, her mother's taste in partners had been less than stellar.

Still, Darin hadn't said anything about their future or what he planned to do once they arrived in Texas. "I hope you understand this, but I have a lot going on in my life," she said. "I've worked really hard to be where I am now. I can't give up my long-term goals for some temporary fling. I can't just be your good-time girl, available whenever you whisk back into town following the latest mission.''

"What if I told you I want more? What if I said I have no intention of leaving you again?''

The words echoed in her brain and headed straight for her heart. "I don't understand what you're saying.''

"Yes, you do.'' He held her tighter. "I've grown tired of living for the moment. I wish to settle down, perhaps have a family.''

"Are you saying you want to do that with me?''

"Yes.''

"Why? Because we've had a few laughs, a few quick tumbles between the sheets. I have to admit, the sex was really good, but—''

"Lovemaking,'' he said sincerely. "We made *love,* Fiona. I made love to you.''

"Then you're saying—''

"That I'm no longer afraid of it.''

"Love?''

"Yes…''

"Then that means—''

"I love you. More than the missions, the adventure. More than my own life. Do you love me, as well?''

How could she possibly deny it? "Didn't I just tell you that in the airport?''

"I would like to hear it again.''

She drew in a deep breath and released it slowly. "I love you, Darin Shakir.''

He kissed her then, tenderly, sweetly, capturing Fiona's heart so firmly, so completely, that the tears tried to make another appearance.

When they parted, he said, "I would be honored to have you as my wife. I would be willing to remain here until you complete your schooling. After that, if you will allow it, I would build you an inn so that you might realize your dreams. It is the least I could do since you have helped me realize mine.''

Darn the tears, Fiona thought, as they came without mercy, rolling down her chin and onto her T-shirt.

"I have made you cry," he said as he wiped one tear away with his thumb. "I never intended to do that."

"Good tears," Fiona said, followed by an annoying sob.

"Then you will consider my proposal?"

She shrugged, then laughed from the joy of the moment. From the purest love shining in Darin's dark eyes. "Oh, why not. I've never been to Texas. But I do have a few conditions."

He frowned. "I am almost afraid to ask what those might be."

"Just a simple things. First, I have to bring Lottie because I would never leave her behind. Second, we have to drive because I refuse to fly. And third, I want you to make sure we have at least a year's supply of condoms, bright colors optional."

Darin laughed then, a deep rich sound as he picked her up and spun her around before planting her back on her feet. "Alexander Kent spoke of a place in Las Vegas where we can be married."

Fiona released his shoulders only long enough to streak a hand over her eyes, to swipe away the remaining tears she no longer needed. "There's a wedding chapel on every corner. But are you really sure this is what you want?"

His expression turned serious. "More than I have wanted anything in a very long time. I would also like to have children, but not before we have a chance to see the world together."

"I would love to have some kids, too." She tucked his hair behind his ears and smiled. "So I guess this means we're in for some more adventure together."

"As long as it involves only the adventure we find in bed."

"You've got a deal. But what are you going to do with your time if you retire from active criminal chasing?"

"Aside from making love to you on a regular basis, I am

going to raise horses. Perhaps cattle. After we return from our very lengthy honeymoon. In Paris.''

"Paris? First you're going to have to get me on a plane.''

He pulled her closer. "If you'll recall, I have ways to do that. Very pleasurable ways. Anything your heart desires.''

Fiona's heart only desired one thing at that moment—to be with her dark stranger, the sheikh in disguise, from this point forward.

Epilogue

Fiona Powers Shakir had landed on Planet Machismo smack dab in the middle of a regular manfest. No doubt about it, the members of the elite Texas Cattleman's Club had macho—and obviously fertility—down to a fine art. She wouldn't doubt it one bit if all they had to do was hang their pants on a bedpost to get a woman pregnant. Which reminded Fiona to make sure Darin kept his trousers in the closet. Not that she didn't want to have a child, but not until she'd had plenty of time alone with him, at least another five years or so, or until the inn-in-progress was well established. But boy, she would sure get in plenty of practice in the meantime if she had anything to say about it.

As they passed through the doors of the hallowed TCC headquarters, Darin introduced Fiona to several of the members, both old and new. They had beautiful wives, equally beautiful children and names like Dakota and Hank and Aaron, too many to remember right now. But at least she had no trouble remembering Darin's cousin's name who greeted them both with a smile. Since their arrival in Royal two weeks ago, Fiona had spent quite a bit of time with Ben and his wife, Jamie, along with their newborn son and lovely little girl—when she wasn't spending time in bed with her husband, doing things that would make Texas bluebonnets wilt in the height of spring.

She hadn't experienced the beauty of the famed state flowers that had withered away before the first heat wave hit with a vengeance. Fiona couldn't say that she blamed them. The arid June temperatures, typical of a Texas summer, threatened to melt her makeup. Not that the scorching weather mattered all that much, since she'd spent most of her time here indoors. However, she was growing rather warm every time she glanced at her debonair husband as they walked out of the building and onto to the back lawn, hand in hand, before entering an elaborate tent—a massive, white air-conditioned tent, draped with twinkling lights and housing rows of linen-covered circular tables for the guests. And there were plenty of guests, along with several silver trays containing every food imaginable set out on banquet tables lining the perimeters of the tent. In the center of the area sat two identical wedding cakes draped in yellow sugar daisies topped with miniature cowboys primed to kiss their miniature brides, a pair of tiny gold boots circled by two gold bands suspended over their heads.

The wedding reception was in honor of Natalie and Travis Whelan, as well as Ryan and Carrie Evans. Both couples had married in the nearby chapel in a private ceremony an hour before. Both women were now joined with Cattleman's Club members, as was Fiona, and looked mighty proud of their mates.

Mighty proud? Only a brief time in Royal and Fiona was already thinking in Texas speak.

Like the wives who had gone before her, Fiona now knew the true purpose of the influential organization. The mantra, etched in white icing on the massive chocolate grooms' cake, said it all: Peace, Justice, Leadership. This diverse group of men—gorgeous, wealthy men—had devoted their time to pursuing the worst of the worst offenders, risking life and limb, and along the way usually falling in love. Or so it had been for the six members involved in the latest mission, as Darin had explained to her earlier.

Darin had also explained that it was Natalie who had shown up in the local diner with a brand-new baby and no memory of where she had been or where she was going. Travis's baby, as it had turned out, bringing the couple back together again, this time for all time. Ryan and Carrie—Travis's little sister—had known each other for years but it wasn't until the nasty Roman Birkenfeld entered the picture and kidnapped Carrie that they'd acknowledged their feelings ran deeper than mere affection. Two wonderful love stories, but as far as Fiona was concerned, neither topped hers and Darin's—a mistaken identity, knife wounds and a deadly doctor in drag. Or at least none were quite as off-the-wall.

Darin guided Fiona to the cake table where wedding parties were now standing, the grooms mugging for the camera while the brides stood by, feigning impatience when they weren't laughing. Fiona had met the other three couples now approaching the table—Alexander Kent and his wife, Stephanie, Clint and Tara Andover and David and Marissa Sorrenson, all newlyweds, same as Fiona and Darin.

The wives exchanged greetings and smiles; the men exchanged handshakes and innuendo. Fiona had experienced nothing but kindness since her arrival in Royal, and she looked forward to building a future here with her exceptional, supersexy husband.

Travis raised his glass of champagne while the attendees gathered round to hear the toast. "To health, happiness and love," he said as he gazed at Natalie, who wore the most beautiful cap-sleeved lace dress that enhanced the soft tone of her olive complexion.

"Here, here," Ryan added as he looked with love at Carrie, whose hair was almost the same color as Fiona's, her satin, strapless gown a soft shade of champagne. "And to headstrong women who are hell-bent to keep us in line. May they all succeed.''

The crowd laughed and applauded their approval while David grabbed the microphone from Travis before he could say anything else. ''Since this is such a damn happy day, I need to make an announcement.'' He hugged Marissa to his side and gave her a devastating smile. ''We're going to have a baby.''

The attendees began to applaud when Travis snatched the microphone from David and lifted a hand to silence them. ''So as not to be outdone by my friend here, Natalie's pregnant again, too.''

Fertility ran amok, Fiona thought with a smile.

More cheers rose from the crowd, and a lot of back slapping ensued. Darin circled his arms around Fiona from behind and pulled her against him, bending his head until his warm lips rested at her ear. ''Are you ready to leave now?''

Fiona looked back at him and saw the familiar fire in his eyes. ''Wouldn't that be rude? We haven't been here that long.''

He slid his palm down the side of the coral satin gown, over the curve of her hip then back up again to her waist. ''True, but this dress has turned my thoughts to another kind of celebration where we are not in need of clothing.''

''But you look so handsome in your tux.'' And he did, so handsome that she wanted to find a back room and show him exactly how much she appreciated it. However, she didn't dare tell him that or he would have her out of there, lickety-split, in search of a broom closet.

''I would prefer to remove our clothing soon. Perhaps we should find somewhere on the premises to do that very thing.''

Mind reader. ''You're very wicked, Sheikh Shakir. We've already spent so much time holed up in our room at the Royalton Hotel, what would people think if we slip away now for a little horizontal mambo in the bathroom?''

He brushed her hair aside and kissed her neck. ''They would think that I am a very wise man.''

"And virile," she added when he pressed against her, letting her know loud and very clear that he was up for the challenge. "So just keep your pants on until we have some place safe to put them."

He turned her around to face him. "Some place safe?"

She grinned. "Never mind."

His expression went oddly somber. "Are you happy, Fiona?"

"Very."

"You have no regrets?"

"Only one."

Concern darkened his eyes, made Fiona melt inside. "Then tell me. I will do everything in my power to give you whatever you need."

She circled her arms around his waist, not caring who was watching their public display of affection. "I regret that I wasted all morning picking out wallpaper for the inn's lobby instead of keeping you in bed until noon."

His expression softened with relief. "There is always tonight."

"And tomorrow we leave for our honeymoon."

"An adventure in Paris."

"If you can convince me to get on that plane."

"Do you trust me?" he asked.

"With my life. With all my heart." Exactly what she'd said to him when he'd asked that same question during their vows in the Vegas chapel a month ago. Exactly what she would tell him every day of their lives. And when she was once again in his arms, she would tell him how much she loved him. How much she cherished what they had found together, despite their fears...and in some ways because of those fears.

For a small-town girl with big time-dreams, Fiona Powers had definitely hit the jackpot. The best dream was holding her in his arms.

*   *   *   *   *

If you enjoyed what you just read,
then we've got an offer you can't resist!

Take 2 bestselling love stories FREE!

Plus get a FREE surprise gift!

Clip this page and mail it to Silhouette Reader Service™

IN U.S.A.
3010 Walden Ave.
P.O. Box 1867
Buffalo, N.Y. 14240-1867

IN CANADA
P.O. Box 609
Fort Erie, Ontario
L2A 5X3

YES! Please send me 2 free Silhouette Desire® novels and my free surprise gift. After receiving them, if I don't wish to receive anymore, I can return the shipping statement marked cancel. If I don't cancel, I will receive 6 brand-new novels every month, before they're available in stores! In the U.S.A., bill me at the bargain price of $3.57 plus 25¢ shipping and handling per book and applicable sales tax, if any*. In Canada, bill me at the bargain price of $4.24 plus 25¢ shipping and handling per book and applicable taxes**. That's the complete price and a savings of at least 10% off the cover prices—what a great deal! I understand that accepting the 2 free books and gift places me under no obligation ever to buy any books. I can always return a shipment and cancel at any time. Even if I never buy another book from Silhouette, the 2 free books and gift are mine to keep forever.

225 SDN DNUP
326 SDN DNUQ

Name	(PLEASE PRINT)	
Address	Apt.#	
City	State/Prov.	Zip/Postal Code

* Terms and prices subject to change without notice. Sales tax applicable in N.Y.
** Canadian residents will be charged applicable provincial taxes and GST.
  All orders subject to approval. Offer limited to one per household and not valid to
  current Silhouette Desire® subscribers.
  ® are registered trademarks of Harlequin Books S.A., used under license.

DES02   ©1998 Harlequin Enterprises Limited

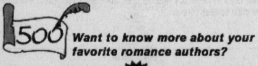

COMING NEXT MONTH

#1579 THE BOSS MAN'S FORTUNE—Kathryn Jensen
Dynasties: The Danforths
Errant heiress Katie Fortune had left home and her oppressive lifestyle
behind and began anew—as secretary to Ian Danforth. The renowned
playboy was a genius in the boardroom. But it was his bedroom
manner that Katie couldn't stop fantasizing about….

#1580 THE LAST GOOD MAN IN TEXAS—Peggy Moreland
The Tanners of Texas
She'd come to Tanner's Crossing looking for her family. What
Macy Keller found was Rory Tanner, unapologetic ladies' man. Rory
agreed to help with Macy's search—to keep an eye on her. But as the
sexual tension began to hum between them, it became difficult to keep
his *hands* off her!

#1581 SHUT UP AND KISS ME—Sara Orwig
Stallion Pass: Texas Knights
Sexy lawyer Savannah Clay was unlike any woman he'd ever known.
Mike Remington hadn't believed she'd take him up on his marriage
proposal—if only for the sake of the baby he'd inherited. Falling into
bed with the feisty blonde was inevitable; it was falling in love that
Mike was worried about….

#1582 REDWOLF'S WOMAN—Laura Wright
When Ava Thompson had left Paradise, Texas, four years ago, she'd
carried with her a little secret. But her daughter was not so little
anymore. Unsuspecting dad Jared Redwolf was blindsided by the
truth—and shaken by the power Ava had over him still. Could the
passion they shared see them through?

#1583 STORM OF SEDUCTION—Cindy Gerard
Tonya Griffin was a photographer of the highest repute…and
Web Tyler wanted her work to grace the pages of his new magazine.
But Web also had other plans for the earthy beauty…and they didn't
involve work, but the most sensual pleasures.

#1584 AT ANY PRICE—Margaret Allison
Kate Devonworth had a little problem. Her small-town paper needed
a big-time loan, and her childhood crush turned wealthy investor
Jack Reilly was just the man to help. Kate resolved to keep things
between them strictly business…until she saw the look in his eyes.
A look that matched the desire inside her….

SDCNM0404